PARDNERS

REX E. BEACH

1st WORLD
LIBRARY
Literary Society

PARDNERS

REX E. BEACH

© 1st World Library – Literary Society, 2005
PO Box 2211
Fairfield, IA 52556
www.1stworldlibrary.org
First Edition

LCCN: 2004195667

Softcover ISBN: 1-4218-0482-4
Hardcover ISBN: 1-4218-0382-8
eBook ISBN: 1-4218-0582-0

Purchase *"Pardners"*
as a traditional bound book at:
www.1stWorldLibrary.org/purchase.asp?ISBN=1-4218-0482-4

1st World Library Literary Society is a nonprofit
organization dedicated to promoting literacy by:

- Creating a free internet library accessible from any
  computer worldwide.
- Hosting writing competitions and offering book
  publishing scholarships.

Pardners
contributed by Tim, Ed & Rodney
in support of
1st World Library Literary Society

CONTENTS

PARDNERS

"Most all the old quotations need fixing," said Joyce in tones forbidding dispute. "For instance, the guy that alluded to marriages germinating in heaven certainly got off on the wrong foot. He meant pardnerships. The same works ain't got capacity for both, no more'n you can build a split-second stop-watch in a stone quarry. No, sir! A true pardnership is the sanctifiedest relation that grows, is, and has its beans, while any two folks of opposite sect can marry and peg the game out some way. Of course, all pardnerships ain't divine. To every one that's heaven borned there's a thousand made in -. There goes them cussed dogs again!"

He dove abruptly at the tent flap, disappearing like a palmed coin, while our canvas structure reeled drunkenly at his impact. The sounds of strife without rose shrilly into blended agony, and the yelps of Keno melted away down the gulch in a rapid and rabid diminuendo.

Inasmuch as I had just packed out from camp in a loose pair of rubber boots, and was nursing two gall blisters, I did not feel called upon to emulate this energy of arbitration, particularly in bare feet.

"That black malamoot is a walking delegate for strife," he remarked, returning. "Sometime I'll lose my temper

- and that's the kind of pardners me and Justus Morrow was."

Never more do I interrupt the allegory of my mate, no matter how startling its structure. He adventures orally when and in the manner the spirit calls, without rote, form, or tone production. Therefore I kicked my blistered heels in the air and grunted aimless encouragement.

"I was prospectin' a claim on Caribou Creek, and had her punched as full of holes as a sponge cake, when the necessity of a change appealed to me. I was out of everything more nourishing than hope and one slab of pay-streaked bacon, when two tenderfeet 'mushed' up the gulch, and invited themselves into my cabin to watch me pan. It's the simplest thing known to science to salt a tenderfoot, so I didn't have no trouble in selling out for three thousand dollars.

"You see, they couldn't kick, 'cause some of us 'old timers' was bound to get their money anyhow - just a question of time; and their inexperience was cheap at the price. Also, they was real nice boys, and I hated to see 'em fall amongst them crooks at Dawson. It was a short-horned triumph, though. Like the Dead Sea biscuits of Scripture, it turned to ashes in my mouth. It wasn't three days later that they struck it; right in my last shaft, within a foot of where I quit diggin'. They rocked out fifty ounces first day. When the news filtered to me, of course, I never made no holler. I couldn't - that is, honestly - but I bought a six hundred dollar grub stake, loaded it aboard a dory, and - having instructed the trader regarding the disposition of my mortal, drunken remains, I fanned through that camp like a prairie fire shot in the sirloin with a hot wind.

"Of course, it wasn't such a big spree; nothing gaudy or Swedelike; but them that should know, claimed it was a model of refinement. Yes, I have got many encomiums on its general proportions and artistic finish. One hundred dollars an hour for twenty-four hours, all in red licker, confined to and in me and my choicest sympathizers. I reckon all our booze combined would have made a fair sluice-head. Anyhow, I woke up considerable farther down the dim vistas of time and about the same distance down the Yukon, in the bottom of my dory, seekin' new fields at six miles an hour. The trader had follered my last will and testament scrupulous, even to coverin' up my legs.

"That's how I drifted into Rampart City, and Justus Morrow.

"This here town was the same as any new camp; a mile long and eighteen inches wide, consisting of saloons, dance-halls, saloons, trading-posts, saloons, places to get licker, and saloons. Might not have been so many dancehalls and trading-posts as I've mentioned, and a few more saloons.

"I dropped into a joint called The Reception, and who'd I see playing 'bank' but 'Single Out' Wilmer, the worst gambler on the river. Mounted police had him on the woodpile in Dawson, then tied a can on him. At the same table was a nice, tender Philadelphia squab, 'bout fryin' size, and while I was watching, Wilmer pulls down a bet belonging to it. That's an old game.

"'Pardon me,' says the broiler; 'you have my checks.'

"'What?' growls 'Single Out;' 'I knowed this game before you quit nursin', Bright Eyes. I can protect my own bets.'

"'That's right,' chimes the dealer, who I seen was 'Curly' Budd, Wilmer's pardner.

"'Lord!' thinks I, 'there's a pair to draw to.'

"'Do you really think you had ought to play this? It's a man's game,' says Wilmer nasty.

"I expected to see the youngster dog it. Nothin' of the kind.

"'That's my bet!' he says again, and I noticed something dry in his voice, like the rustle of silk.

"Single Out just looks black and snarls at the dealer.

"'Turn the cards!'

"'Oh, very well,' says the chechako, talking like a little girl.

"Somebody snickered and, thinks I 'there's sprightly doin's hereabouts. I'll tarry a while and see 'em singe the fowl. I like the smell of burning pin feathers; it clears my head.'

"Over in the far corner was another animal in knee panties, riggin' up one of these flash-light, snappy-shot, photograft layouts. I found afterwards that he done it for a living; didn't work none, just strayed around as co-respondent for an English newspaper syndicate, taking pictures and writing story things. I didn't pay much attention to him hiding under his black cloth, 'cause the faro-table was full of bets, and it's hard to follow the play. Well, bye-and-bye Wilmer shifted another stack belonging to the Easterner.

"The lad never begged his pardon nor nothin'. His fist just shot out and landed on the nigh corner of Wilmer's jaw, clean and fair, and 'Single Out' done as pretty a headspin as I ever see - considering that it was executed in a cuspidore. 'Twas my first insight into the amenities of football. I'd like to see a whole game of it. They say it lasts an hour and a half. Of all the cordial, why-how-do-you-do mule kicks handed down in rhyme and story, that wallop was the adopted daddy.

"When he struck, I took the end of the bar like a steeplechaser, for I seen 'Curly' grab at the drawer, and I have aversions to witnessing gun plays from the front end. The tenderfoot riz up in his chair, and snatchin' a stack of reds in his off mit, dashed 'em into 'Curly's' face just as he pulled trigger. It spoiled his aim, and the boy was on to him like a mountain lion, follerin' over the table, along the line of least resistance.

"It was like takin' a candy sucker from a baby. 'Curly' let go of that 'six' like he was plumb tired of it, and the kid welted him over the ear just oncet. Then he turned on the room; and right there my heart went out to him. He took in the line up at a sweep of his lamps:

"'Any of you gentlemen got ideas on the subject?' he says, and his eyes danced like waves in the sunshine.

"It was all that finished and genteel that I speaks up without thinkin', 'You for me pardner!'

"Just as I said it, there come a swish and flash as if a kag of black powder had changed its state of bein'. I s'pose everybody yelled and dodged except the picture man. He says, 'Thank you, gents; very pretty tableau.'

"It was the first flash-light I ever see, and all I recall now is a panorama of starin' eyeballs and gaping mouths. When it seen it wasn't torpedoed, the population begin crawlin' out from under chairs and tables. Men hopped out like toads in a rain.

"I crossed the boy's trail later that evening; found him watchin' a dance at the Gold Belt. The photografter was there, too, and when he'd got his dog-house fixed, he says:

"'Everybody take pardners, and whoop her up. I want this picture for the *Weekly*. Get busy, you, there!" We all joined in to help things; the orchestra hit the rough spots, and we went highfalutin' down the centre, to show the English race how our joy pained us, and that life in the Klondyke had the Newport whirl, looking like society in a Siwash village. He got another good picture.

"Inside of a week, Morrow and I had joined up. We leased a claim and had our cabin done, waiting for snow to fall so's to sled our grub out to the creek. He took to me like I did to him, and he was an educated lad, too. Somehow, though, it hadn't gone to his head, leaving his hands useless, like knowledge usually does.

"One day, just before the last boat pulled down river, Mr. Struthers, the picture man, come to us - R. Alonzo Struthers, of London and 'Frisco, he was - and showin' us a picture, he says:

"'Ain't that great? Sunday supplements! Full page!

Big display! eh?'

"It sure was. 'Bout 9x9, and showing every detail of the Reception saloon. There was 'Single Out' analyzing the cuspidore and 'Curly' dozin', as contorted and well-done as a pretzel. There was the crowd hiding in the corners, and behind the faro-table stood the kid, one hand among the scattered chips and cards, the other dominating the layout with 'Curley's' 'six.' It couldn't have looked more natural if we'd posed for it. It was a bully likeness, I thought, too, till I seen myself glaring over the bar. All that showed of William P. Joyce, bachelor of some arts and plenty of science, late of Dawson, was the white of his eyes. And talkin' of white - say, I looked like I had washing hung out. Seemed like the draught had riz my hair up, too.

"'Nothing like it ever seen,' continues Struthers. 'I'll call it 'The Winning Card,' or 'At Bay,' or something like that. Feature it as a typical Klondyke card game. I'll give you a two-page write-up. Why, it's the greatest thing I ever did!'

"'I'm sorry,' says Morrow, thoughtful, 'but you musn't run it.'

"'What! says he, and I thinks, 'Oh, Lord! There goes my only show to get perpetufied in ink.'

"'I can't let you use it. My wife might see it.'

"'Your wife!' says I. 'Are you married, pardner?'

"'Yes, I'm married,' and his voice sounded queer. 'I've got a boy - too, see.'

"He took a locket from his flannel shirt and opened it. A curly-headed, dimpled little youngster laughed out at me.

"'Well, I'm d -!' and then I took off my hat, for in the other side was a woman - and, gentlemen, she *was* a woman! When I seen her it made me feel blushy and ashamed. Gee! She was a stunner. I just stared at her till Struthers looked over my shoulder, and says, excited:

"'Why, it's Olive Troop, the singer!'

"'Not any more,' says Morrow, smiling.

"'Oh! So you're the fellow she gave up her art for? I knew her on the stage.'

"Something way deep down in the man grated on me, but the kid was lookin' at the picture and never noticed, while hunger peered from his face.

"'You can't blame me,' he says finally. 'She'd worry to death if she saw that picture. The likeness is too good. You might substitute another face on my shoulders; that can be done, can't it?'

"'Why, sure; dead easy, but I'll not run it at all if you feel that way,' says the artist.

"Then, Morrow resumes, 'You'll be in Denver this fall, Struthers, eh? Well, I want you to take a letter to her. She'll be glad to see an old friend like you, and to hear from me. Tell her I'm well and happy, and that I'll make a fortune, sure. Tell her, too, that there won't be any mail out of here till spring.'

"Now, I don't claim no second sight in the matter of female features: I ain't had no coachin'; not even as much as the ordinary, being raised on a bottle, but I've studied the ornery imprints of men's thoughts, over green tables and gun bar'ls, till I can about guess whether they've drawed four aces or an invite to a funeral. I got another flash from that man I didn't like, though his words were hearty. He left, soon after, on the last boat.

"Soon as ever the ground froze we began to sink. In those days steam thawers wasn't dreamed of, so we slid wood down from the hills, and burned the ground with fires. It's slow work, and we didn't catch bed-rock till December, but when we did we struck it right. Four feet of ten-cent dirt was what she averaged. Big? Well, I wonder! It near drove Morrow crazy.

"'Billy, old boy, this means I'll see her next summer!'

"Whenever he mentioned her name, he spoke like a man in church or out of breath. Somehow it made me feel like takin' off my cap - forty below at that, and my ears freeze terrible willing since that winter on the Porcupine.

"That evening, when I wasn't looking, he sneaked the locket out of his shirt and stared at it, famished. Then he kissed it, if you might rehabilitate such a scandalous, hold-fast-for-the-corner performance by that name.

"'I must let her know right away,' says he. 'How can I do it?'

"'We can hire a messenger, and send him to Dawson,' says I. 'Everybody in camp will pay five dollars a letter, and he can bring back the outside mail. They have monthly service from there to the coast. He'll make the trip in ninety days, so you'll get news from home by the first of March. Windy Jim will go. He'd leave a good job and a warm camp any time to hit the trail. Just hitch up the dogs, crack a whip, and yell 'Mush on!' and he'll get the snow-shoe itch, and water at the mouth for hardship.'

"Not being house-broke and tame myself, I ain't authority on the joys of getting mail from home, but, next to it, I judge, comes writing to your family. Anyhow, the boy shined up like new money, and there was from one to four million pages in his hurried note. I don't mean to say that he was grouchy at any time. No, sir! He was the nickel-plated sunbeam of the whole creek. Why, I've knowed him to do the cooking for two weeks at a stretch, and never kick - and *wash the dishes, too*, - which last, as anybody knows, is crucifyin'er than that smelter test of the three Jews in the Scripture. Underneath all of his sunshine, though, I saw hints of an awful, aching, devilish, starvation. It made me near hate the woman that caused it.

"He was a wise one, too. I've seen him stirring dog-feed with one hand and spouting 'Gray's Elegy' with the other. I picked up a heap of knowledge from him, for he had American history pat. One story I liked particular was concerning the origin of placer mining in this country, about a Greaser, Jason Somebody, who got the gold fever and grub-staked a mob he called the Augerknots - carpenters, I judge, from the mess they made of it. They chartered a schooner and prospected along Asy Miner, wherever that is. I never seen any boys from there, but the formation was wrong, like Texas, probably, 'cause they sort of drifted into the sheep business. Of course, that was a long ways back, before the '49 rush, but the way he told it was great.

"Well, two weeks after Windy left we worked out of that rich spot and drifted into barren ground. Instead of a fortune, we'd sunk onto the only yellow spot in the whole claim. We cross-cut in three places, and never raised a colour, but we kept gophering around till March, in hopes.

"'Why did I write that letter?' he asked one day. 'I'd give anything to stop it before it gets out. Think of her disappointment when she hears I'm broke!'

"'Nobody can't look into the ground,' says I. 'I don't mind losin' out myself, for I've done it for twenty years and I sort of like it now, but I'm sorry for the girl.'

"'It means another whole season,' he says. 'I wanted to see them this summer, or bring them in next fall.'

"'Sufferin' sluice-boxes! Are you plumb daffy? Bring a woman into the Yukon - and a little baby.'

"'She'd follow me anywhere. She's awful proud; proud as a Kentucky girl can be, and those people would make your uncle Lucifer look like a cringing cripple, but she'd live in an Indian hut with me.'

"'Sure! And follerin' out the simile, nobody but a Siwash would let her. If she don't like some other feller better while you're gone, what're you scared about?'

"He never answered; just looked at me pityfyin', as much as to say, 'Well, you poor, drivelin, old polyp!'

"One day Denny, the squaw-man, drove up the creek:

"'Windy Jim is back with the mail,' says he, and we hit for camp on the run. Only fifteen mile, she is, but I was all in when we got there, keepin' up with Justus. His eyes outshone the snow-glitter and he sang - all the time he wasn't roasting me for being so slow - claimed I was active as a toad-stool. A man ain't got no license to excite hisself unless he's struck pay dirt - or got a divorce.

"'Gi'me my mail, quick!' he says to Windy, who had tinkered up a one-night stand post-office and dealt out letters, at five dollars per let.'

"'Nothing doing,' says Windy.

"'Oh, yes there is,' he replies, still smiling; 'she writes me every week.'

"'I got all there was at Dawson,' Windy give back, 'and there ain't a thing for you!'

"I consider the tragedy of this north country lies in its mail service. Uncle Sam institutes rural deliveries, so the bolomen can register poisoned arrowheads to the Igorrotes in exchange for recipes to make roulade of naval officer, but his American miners in Alaska go shy on home news for eight months every year.

"That was the last mail we had till June.

"When the river broke we cleaned up one hundred and eighty-seven dollars' worth of lovely, yellow dust, and seven hundred and thirty-five dollars in beautiful yellow bills from the post.

Rex E. Beach

"The first boat down from Dawson brought mail, and I stood beside him when he got his. He shook so he held on to the purser's window. Instead of a stack of squares overrun with female chiropody, there was only one for him - a long, hungry sport, with indications of a law firm in the northwest corner. It charmed him like a rattler. He seemed scared to open it. Two or three times he tried and stopped.

"'They're dead,' thinks I; and, sure enough, when he'd looked, I knew it was so, and felt for his hand. Sympathy don't travel by word of mouth between pardners. It's the grip of the hand or the look of the eye.

"'What cause?' says I.

"He turned, and s'help me, I never want to see the like again. His face was plumb grey and dead, like wet ashes, while his eyes scorched through, all dry and hot. Lines was sinkin' into it as I looked.

"'It's worse,' says he, 'unless it's a joke.' He handed me the dope: 'In re Olive Troop Morrow *vs.* Justus Morrow,' and a letter stating that out of regard for her feelings, and bein' a gentleman, he wasn't expected to cause a scandal, but to let her get the divorce by default. No explanation; no word from her; nothing.

"God knows what that boy suffered the next few weeks, but he fought it out alone. She was proud, but he was prouder. Her silence hurt him the worst, of course; but what could he do? Go to her? Fine! Both of us broke and in debt. Also, there's such a thing as diggin' deep enough to scrape the varnish off of a man's self-respect, leavin' it raw and shrinking. No! He done like you or me - let her have her way. He took off the locket and hid it, and I never heard her name mentioned for a year.

"I'd been up creek for a whip-saw one day, and as I came back I heard voices in the cabin. 'Some musher out from town,' thinks I, till something in their tones made me stop in my tracks.

"I could hear the boy's voice, hoarse and throbbing, as though he dragged words out bleeding, then I heard the other one laugh - a nasty, sneering laugh that ended in a choking rattle, like a noose had tightened on his throat.

"I jumped for the door, and rounding the corner, something near took me off my feet; something that shot through the air, all pretty and knickerbockery, with a two-faced cap, and nice brown leggin's. Also, a little camera was harnessed to it by tugs. It arose, displaying the face of R. Alonzo Struthers, black and swollen, with chips stickin' in it where he'd hit the woodpile. He glared at Morrow, and his lips foamed like a crab out of water.

"'I hope I'm not intrudin', I ventures.

"When the kid seen me, he says, soft and weak, like something ailed his palate:

"'Don't let me kill him, Billy.'"

"Struthers spit, and picked splinters forth from his complexion.

"'I told you for your own good. It's common gossip,' says he. 'Everybody is laughing at you, an -'

"Then I done a leap for life for the kid, 'cause the murder light blazed up white in his face, and he moved at the man like he had something serious in view.

"'Run, you idiot!' I yells to Struthers as I jammed the youngster back into the cabin. All of a sudden the gas went out of him and he broke, hanging to me like a baby.

"'It can't be,' he whispers. 'It can't be.' He throwed hisself on to a goods' box, and buried his face in his hands. It gripes me to hear a man cry, so I went to the creek for a pail of water.

"I never heard what Struthers said, but it don't take no Nick Carter to guess.

"That was the fall of the Fryin' Pan strike - do you mind it? Shakespeare George put us on, so me and the kid got in ahead of the stampede. We located one and two above discovery, and by Christmas we had a streak uncovered that was all gold. She was coarse, and we averaged six ounces a day in pick-ups. Man, that *was* ground! I've flashed my candle along the drift face, where it looked like gold had been shot in with a scatter-gun.

"We was cleaned up and had our 'pokes' at the post when the first boat from Dawson smoked 'round the bend.

"Now, in them days, a man's averdupoise was his abstract of title. There was nothing said about records and patentees as long as you worked your ground; but, likewise, when you didn't work it, somebody else usually did. We had a thousand feet of as good dirt as ever laid out in the rain; but there was men around drulin' to snipe it, and I knowed it was risky to leave. However, I saw what was gnawin' at the boy, and if ever a man needed a friend and criminal lawyer, that was the time. According to the zodiac, certain persons, to the complainant unknown, had a mess of trouble comin' up and I wanted to have the bail money handy.

"We jumped camp together. I made oration to the general gnat-bitten populace, from the gang-plank, to the effect that one William P. Joyce, trap, crap, and snap shooter was due to happen back casual most any time, and any lady or gent desirous of witnessing at first hand, a shutzenfest with live targets, could be gratified by infestin' in person or by proxy, the lands, tenements, and hereditaments of me and the kid.

"'Well, we hit the Seattle docks at a canter, him headed for the postal telegraph, me for a fruit-stand. I bought a dollar's worth of everything, from cracker-jack to cantaloupe, reserving the local option of eatin' it there in whole or in part, and returning for more. First fresh fruit in three years. I reckon my proudest hour come when I found, beyond peradventure, that I hadn't forgot the 'Georgy Grind.' What? 'Georgy Grind' consists of feeding rough-hewed slabs of watermelon into your sou' sou'east corner, and squirting a stream of seeds out from the other cardinal points, without stopping or strangling.

"I et and et, and then wallered up to the hotel, sweatin' a different kind of fruit juice from every pore. Not wishing to play any favourites, I'd picked up a basket of tomatoes, a gunny-sack of pineapples, and a peck of green plums on the way. Them plums done the business. I'd orter let bad enough alone. They was non-union, and I begin having trouble with my inside help. Morrow turned in a hurry-up call for the Red Cross, two medical colleges, and the Society of Psycolic Research. Between 'em they diagnosed me as containing everything from 'housemaid's knee' to homesickness of the vital organs, but I *know*. I swallered a plum pit, and it sprouted.

"Next day, when I come out of it, Justus had heard from Denver. His wife had been gone a year, destination unknown. Somebody thought she went to California, so, two days later, we registered at the Palace, and the 'Frisco police begin dreaming of five thousand dollar rewards.

"It was no use, though. One day I met Struthers on Market Street, and he was scared stiff to hear that Morrow was in town. It seems he was night editor of one of the big dailies.

"'Do you know where the girl is?' says I.

"'Yes, she's in New York,' he answers, looking queer, so I hurried back to the hotel.

"As I was explaining to Morrow, a woman passed us in the hall with a little boy. In the dimness, the lad mistook Justus.

"'Oh, papa, papa!" he yells, and grabs him by the knees, laughing and kicking.

"'Ah-h!' my pardner sighs, hoarse as a raven, and quicker'n light he snatched the little shaver to him, then seeing his mistake, dropped him rough. His face went grey again, and he got wabbly at the hinges, so I helped him into the parlour. He had that hungry, Yukon look, and breathed like he was wounded.

"'You come with me,' says I, 'and get your mind off of things. The eastern limited don't leave till midnight. Us to the theatre!'

"It was a swell tepee, all right. Variety house, with moving pictures, and actorbats, and two-ton soubrettes, with Barrios diamonds and hand-painted socks.

"First good show I'd seen in three years, and naturally humour broke out all over me. When joy spreads its wings in my vitals, I sound like a boy with a stick running past a picket-fence. Not so Morrow. He slopped over the sides of his seat, like he'd been spilled into the house.

"Right after the sea-lions, the orchestra spieled some teetery music, and out floats a woman, slim and graceful as an antelope. She had a big pay-dump of brown hair, piled up on her hurricane deck, with eyes that snapped and crinkled at the corners. She single-footed in like a derby colt, and the somnambulists in the front row begin to show cause. Something about her startled me, so I nudged the kid, but he was chin-deep in the plush, with his eyes closed. I marked how drawed and haggard he looked; and then, of a sudden he raised half on to his feet. The girl had begun to sing. Her voice was rich and low, and full of deep, still places, like a mountain stream. ButMorrow! He sunk his fingers into me, and leaned for'rad, starin' as though Paradise had opened for him, while the sweat on his face shone like diamond chips.

"It was the girl of the locket, all right, on the stage

again - in vaudeville.

"Her song bubbled along, rippling over sandy, sunlit gravel bars, and slidin' out through shadowy trout pools beneath the cool, alder thickets, and all the time my pardner sat burning his soul in his eyes, his breath achin' out through his throat. Incidental, his digits was knuckle-deep into the muscular tissue of William P., the gent to the right.

"When she quit, I had to jam him back.

"For an encore she sang a reg'lar American song, with music to it. When she reached the chorus she stopped. Then away up in the balcony sounded the tiny treble of a boy's soprano, sweet as the ring of silver. The audience turned, to a man, and we seen, perched among the newsboys, the littlest, golden-haired young-ster, 'bout the size of your thumb, his eyes glued to the face of his mother on the stage below, pourin' out his lark song, serious and frightened. Twice he done it, while by main stren'th I held his father to the enjoy-ments of a two-dollar orchestra chair.

"'Let us in,' we says, three minutes later, to the stranger at the stage door, but he looked upon us with unwelcome, like the seven-headed hydrant of Holy Writ.

"'It's agin' the rules,' says he. 'You kin wait in the alley with the other Johnnies.'

"I ain't acclimated to the cold disfavour of a stage door, never having soubretted along the bird and bottle route. I was for the layin' on of hands. Moreover, I didn't like the company we was in, 'Johnnies,' by designations of the Irish terrier at the wicket. They smoked ready-made cigarettes, and some of 'em must have measured full eight inches acrost the chest.

"'Let us stroll gently but firmly into, over, and past the remains of this party, to the missus,' says I, but Morrow got seized with the shakes, of a sudden.

"'No, no. We'll wait here.'

"At last she come out, steppin' high. When she moved she rustled and rattled like she wore sandpaper at the ankles.

"Say, she was royal! She carried the youngster in her arms, sound asleep, and it wasn't till she stepped under the gaslight that she seen us.

"'Oh!' she cried, and went white as the lace of her cloak. Then she hugged the kiddie clost to her, standing straight and queenly, her eyes ablaze, her lips moist, and red, and scornful.

"God, she was grand - but him? He looked like a barnacle.

"'Olive!' says he, bull-froggy, and that's all. Just quit like a dog and ate her up by long-distance eyesight. Lord! Nobody would have knowed him for the same man that called the crookedest gamblers on the Yukon, and bolted newspaper men raw. He had ingrowing language. It oozed out through his pores till he dreened like a harvest hand. I'd have had her in my arms in two winks, so that all hell and a policeman couldn't have busted my holt till she'd said she loved me.

"She shrivelled him with a look, the likes of which ain't strayed over the Mason-Dixon line since Lee surrendered, and swept by us, invitin' an' horspitable as an iceberg in a cross sea. Her cab door slammed, and I yanked Morrow out of there, more dead than alive.

"'Let me go home,' says he wearily.

"'You bet!' I snorts. 'It's time you was tucked in. The dew is fallin' and some rude person might accost you. You big slob! There's a man's work to do to-night, and as I don't seem to have no competition in holding the title, I s'pose it's my lead.' I throwed him into a carriage. 'You'd best put on your nighty, and have the maid turn down your light. Sweet dreams, Gussie!' I was plumb sore on him. History don't record no divorce suits in the Stone Age, when a domestic inclined man allus toted a white-oak billy, studded with wire nails, according to the pictures, and didn't scruple to use it, both at home and abroad. Women was hairy, them days, and harder to make love, honour and obey; but principles is undyin'.

"I boarded another cab:

"'Drive me to number -,' giving him the address I'd heard her use.

"'Who is it,' came her voice when I rang the bell.

"'Messenger boy,' I replies, perjuring my vocal cords.

"When she opened the door, I pushed through and closed it behind me.

"'What does this mean?' she cried. 'Help!'

"'Shut up! It means you're killing the best boy in the world, and I want to know why.'

"'Who are you?'

"'I'm Bill Joyce, your husband's pardner. Old Tarantula Bill, that don't fear no man, woman, or child that roams the forest. I'm here to find what ails you -'

"'Leave this house, sir!'

"'Well, not to any extent. You're a good girl; I knowed it when I first seen your picture. Now, I want you to tell me -'

"'Insolent! Shall I call the police?' Her voice was icy, and she stood as solid as stone.

"'Madam, I'm as gentle as a jellyfish, and peaceful to a fault, but if you raise a row before I finish my talk I'll claim no responsibility over what occurs to the first eight or ten people that intrudes,' and I drawed my skinnin' knife, layin' it on the planner. 'Philanthropy is raging through my innards, and two loving hearts need joining!'

"'I don't love him,' she quotes, like a phonograft, ignoring my cutlery.

"'I'll take exception to that ruling,' and I picks up a picture of Justus she'd dropped as I broke in. She never batted an eye.

"'I nursed that lad through brain fever, when all he could utter was your name.'

"'Has he been sick?' The first sign of spring lit up her peaks.

"'Most dead. Notice of the divorce done it. He's in bad shape yet.' Morrow never had a sick day in his life, but I stomped both feet on the soft pedal, and pulled out the tremulo stop.

"'Oh! Oh!' Her voice was soft, though she still stood like a birch.

"'Little girl,' I laid a hand on her shoulder. 'We both love that boy. Come, now, what is the matter?'

"She flashed up like powder.

"'Matter? I thought he was a gentleman, even though he didn't love me; that he had a shred of honour, at least. But no! He went to Alaska and made a fortune. Then he squandered it, drinking, fighting, gambling, and frittering it away on women. Bah! Lewd creatures of the dance-halls, too.'

"'Hold up! Your dope sheet is way to the bad. There's something wrong with your libretto. Who told you all that?'

"'Never mind. I have proof. Look at these, and you dare to ask me why I left him?'

"She dragged out some pictures and throwed 'em at me.

"'Ah! Why didn't I let the kid kill him?' says I, through my teeth.

"The first was the gambling-room of the Reception. There stood Morrow with the men under foot; there was the bottles and glasses; the chips and cards, and also the distressful spectacle of Tarantula Bill Joyce, a number twelve man, all gleaming teeth, and rolling eyeballs, inserting hisself into a number nine opening, and doing surprising well at it.

"'Look at them. Look at them well,' she gibed.

"The second was the Gold-Belt dance-hall, with the kid cavorting through a drunken orgy of painted ladies, like a bull in a pansy patch. But the other - it took my breath away till I felt I was on smooth ice, with cracks showing. It was the inside of a cabin, after a big 'pot-latch,' displaying a table littered up with fizz bottles and dishes galore. Diamond Tooth Lou stood on a chair, waving kisses and spilling booze from a mug. In the centre stood Morrow with another girl, nestling agin his boosum most horrible lovin'. Gee! It was a home splitter and it left me sparring for wind. The whole thing exhaled an air of debauchery that would make a wooden Indian blush. No one thing in particular; just the general local colour of a thousand-dollar bender.

"'Charming, isn't it?' she sneered.

"'I don't savvy the burro. There's something phony about it. I can explain the other two, but this one - .' Then it come to me in a flash. The man's face was perfect, but he wore knickerbockers! Now, to my personal knowledge, the only being that ever invaded Rampart City in them things was R. Alonzo Struthers.

"'There's secrets of the dark-room that I ain't wise to,'

says I, 'but I feel that this is going to be a bad night for the newspaper enterprise of 'Frisco if it don't explain. I'll fetch the man that busted your Larrys and Peanuts.'

"'Our what?' says she.

"'Larrys and Peanuts - that's Roman. The kid told me all about 'em. They're sort of little cheap gods!'

"'Will you ever go?' she snapped. 'I don't need your help. Tell him I hate him!' She stamped her foot, and the iron come into her again till the pride of all Kentucky blazed in her eyes.

"She couldn't understand my explanations no more than I could, so I ducked. As I backed out the door, though, I seen her crumple up and settle all of a heap on the floor. She certainly did hate that man scandalous.

"I'm glad some editors work nights. Struthers wasn't overjoyed at my call, particular, as I strayed in with two janitors dangling from me. They said he was busy and couldn't be interrupted, and they seemed to insist on it.'

"'It's a bully night,' says I, by way of epigram, unhooking the pair of bouncers. "'You wouldn't like me to take you ridin' perhaps?'

"'Are you drunk, or crazy?' says he. 'What do you mean by breaking into my office? I can't talk to you; we're just going to press.'

"'I'd like to stay and watch it,' says I, 'but I've got a news item for you.' At the same time I draws my skinner and lays it on the back of his neck, tempting. Steel, in the lamp-light, is discouraging to some temperaments. One of the body-guards was took with urgent business, and left a streamer of funny noises behind him, while the other gave autumn-leaf imitations in the corner. Struthers looked like a dose of seasickness on a sour stomach.

"Get your hat. Quick!' I jobbed him, gentle and encouraging.

"Age allus commands respect. Therefore the sight of a six-foot, grizzled Klondiker in a wide hat, benevolently prodding the night editor in the short ribs and apple sauce, with eight bright and chilly inches, engendered a certain respect in the reportorial staff.

"'You're going to tell Mrs. Morrow all about the pretty pictures,' I says, like a father.

"'Let me go, damn you!' he frothed, but I wedged him into a corner of the cab and took off his collar - in strips. It interfered with his breathing, as I couldn't get a holt low enough to regulate his respiration. He kicked out two cab windows, but I bumped his head agin the woodwork, by way of repartee. It was a real pleasure, not to say recreation, experimenting with the noises he made. Seldom I get a neck I give a cuss to squeeze. His was number fifteen at first, by the feel; but I reduced it a quarter size at a time.

"When we got there I helped him out, one hand under his chin, the other back of his ears. I done it as much from regard of the neighbours as animosities to him, for it was the still, medium small hours. I tiptoed in with my treatise on the infamies of photography gurgling under my hand, but at the door I stopped. It was ajar; and there, under the light, I spied Morrow. In his arms I got glimpses of black lace and wavy, brown hair, and a white cheek that he was accomplishing wonders with. They wouldn't have heard a man-hole explosion.

"'He's still fitting to be my pardner,' I thinks, and then I heard Struthers's teeth chatter and grind. I looked at him, and the secret of the whole play came to me.

"Never having known the divine passion, it ain't for me to judge, but I tightened on his voice-box and whispered:

"'You've outlived your period of usefulness, Struthers, and it's time to go. Let us part friends, however.' So I bade him Godspeed from the top step.

"Looking back on the evening now, that adieu was my only mistake. I limped for a week - he had a bottle in his hip pocket."

THE MULE DRIVER AND
THE GARRULOUS MUTE

Bill had finished panning the concentrates from our last clean-up, and now the silver ball of amalgam sizzled and fried on the shovel over the little chip-fire, while we smoked in the sun before the cabin. Removed from the salivating fumes of the quicksilver, we watched the yellow tint grow and brighten in the heat.

"There's two diseases which the doctors ain't got any license to monkey with," began Bill, chewing out blue smoke from his lungs with each word, "and they're both fevers. After they butt into your system they stick crossways, like a swallered toothpick; there ain't any patent medicine that can bust their holt."

I settled against the door-jamb and nodded.

"I've had them both, acute and continuous, since I was old enough to know my own mind and the taste of tobacco; I hold them mainly responsible for my present condition." He mournfully viewed his fever-ridden frame which sprawled a pitiful six-feet-two from the heels of his gum-boots to the grizzled hair beneath his white Stetson.

"The first and most rabid," he continued, "is horse-racing - and t'other is the mining fever, which last is a

Rex E. Beach

heap insidiouser in its action and more lingering in its effect.

"It wasn't long after that deal in the Territory that I felt the symptoms coming on agin, and this time they pinted most emphatic toward prospecting, so me and 'Kink' Martin loaded our kit onto the burros and hit West.

"Kink was a terrible good prospector, though all-fired unlucky and peculiar. Most people called him crazy, 'cause he had fits of goin' for days without a peep.

"Hosstyle and ornery to the whole world; sort of bulging out and exploding with silence, as it were.

"We'd been out in the hills for a week on our first trip before he got one of them death-watch faces on him, and boycotted the English langwidge. I stood for it three days, trying to jolly a grin on to him or rattle a word loose, but he just wouldn't jolt.

"One night we packed into camp tired, hungry, and dying for a good feed.

"I hustled around and produced a supper fit for old Mr. Eppycure. Knowing that Kink had a weakness for strong coffee that was simply a hinge in him, I pounded up about a quart of coffee beans in the corner of a blanket and boiled out a South American liquid that was nothing but the real Arbuckle mud.

"This wasn't no chafing-dish party either, because the wood was wet and the smoke chased me round the fire. Then it blazed up in spurts and fired the bacon-grease, so that when I grabbed the skillet the handle sizzled the life all out of my callouses. I kicked the fire down to a nice bed of coals and then the coffee-pot upset and put it out. Ashes got into the bacon, and - Oh! you know how joyful it is to cook on a green fire when you're dead tired and your hoodoo's on vicious.

"When the 'scoffings' were finally ready, I wasn't in what you might exactly call a mollyfying and tactful mood nor exuding genialness and enthusiasms anyways noticeable."

"I herded the best in camp towards him, watching for a benevolent symptom, but he just dogged it in silence and never changed a hair. That was the limit, so I inquired sort of ominous and gentle, 'Is that coffee strong enough for ye, Mr. Martin?'

"He give a little impecunious grunt, implying, 'Oh! it'll do,' and with that I seen little green specks begin to buck and wing in front of my eyes; reaching back of me, I grabbed the Winchester and throwed it down on him.

"'Now, you laugh, darn you,' I says, 'in a hurry. Just turn it out gleeful and infractious.'

"He stared into the nozzle of that Krupp for a minute, then swallered twice to tune up his reeds, and says, friendly and perlite, but serious and wheezy:

"'Why, what in hell ails you, William?'

"'Laugh, you old dong-beater,' I yells, rising gradually to the occasion, 'or I'll bust your cupola like a blue-rock.'

"'I've got to have merriment,' I says. 'I pine for warmth and genial smiles, and you're due to furnish the sunshine. You emit a few shreds of mirth with expedition or the upper end of your spinal-cord is going to catch cold.'

"Say! his jaws squeaked like a screen door when he loosened, but he belched up a beauty, sort of stagy and artificial it was, but a great help. After that we got to know each other a heap better. Yes, sir; soon after that we got real intimate. He knocked the gun out of my hands, and we began to arbitrate. We plumb ruined that spot for a camping place; rooted it up in furrows, and tramped each other's stummicks out of shape. We finally reached an amicable settlement by me getting him agin a log where I could brand him with the coffee-pot.

"Right there we drawed up a protoplasm, by the terms of which he was to laugh anyways twice at meal-times.

"He told me that he reckoned he was locoed, and always had been since a youngster, when the Injuns run in on them down at Frisbee, the time of the big 'killing.' Kink saw his mother and father both murdered, and other things, too, which was impressive, but not agreeable for a growing child. He had formed a sort of antipathy for Injuns at that time, which he confessed he hadn't rightly been able to overcome.

"Now, he allus found himself planning how to hand Mr. Lo the double cross and avoid complications.

"We worked down into South Western Arizony to a spot about thirty-five miles back of Fort Walker and struck a prospect. Sort of a teaser it was, but worth working on. We'd just got nicely started when Kink comes into camp one day after taking a passiar around the butte for game, and says:

"'The queerest thing happened to me just now, Kid.'

"'Well, scream it at me,' I says, sort of smelling trouble in the air.

"'Oh! It wasn't much,' says he. 'I was just working down the big canyon over there after a deer when I seen two feather-dusters coming up the trail. I hid behind a rock, watching 'em go past, and I'm durned if my gun didn't go off accidental and plumb ruin one of 'em. Then I looks carefuller and seen it wasn't no feather-duster at all - nothing but an Injun.'

"'What about the other one?'

"'That's the strangest part,' says Kink. 'Pretty soon the other one turns and hits the back-trail like he'd forgot something; then I seen him drop off his horse, too, sudden and all togetherish. I'm awful careless with this here gun,' he says. I hate to see a man laugh from his tonsils forrard, the way he did. It ain't humorous.

"'See here,' I says, 'I ain't the kind that finds fault with my pardner, nor saying this to be captious and critical of your play; but don't you know them Cochises ain't on the warpath? Them Injuns
has been on their reservation for five years, peaceable, domesticated, and eating from the hand. This means trouble."

"'My old man didn't have no war paint on him one day back at

Rex E. Beach

Frisbee,' whispers Kink, and his voice sounded puckered up and dried, 'and my mother wasn't so darned quarrelsome, either.'

"Then I says, 'Well! them bodies has got to be hid, or we'll have the tribe and the bluebellies from the fort a scouring these hills till a red-bug couldn't hide.'

"'To hell with 'em,' says Kink. 'I've done all I'm going to for 'em. Let the coyotes finish the job.'

"'No, siree,' I replies. 'I don't blame you for having a prejudice agin savages, but *my* parents is still robust and husky, and I have an idea that they'd rather see me back on the ranch than glaring through the bars for life. I'm going over to bury the meat.'

"Off I went, but when I slid down the gulch, I only found one body. T'other had disappeared. You can guess how much time I lost getting back to camp.

"'Kink,' I says, 'we're a straddle of the raggedest proposition in this country. One of your dusters at this moment is jamming his cayuse through the horizon between here and the post. Pretty soon things is going to bust loose. 'Bout to-morrer evening we'll be eating hog-bosom on Uncle Sam.'

"'Well! Well!' says Kink, 'ain't that a pity. Next time I'll conquer my natural shyness and hold a post-mortem with a rock.'

"'There won't be no next time, I reckon,' I says, "cause we can't make it over into Mexico without being caught up. They'll nail us sure, seeing as we're the only white men for twenty-five miles around.'

"'I'd rather put up a good run than a bad stand, anyhow,' says he, 'and I allows, furthermore, there's going to be some hard trails to foller and a tolable disagreeable fight before I pleads 'not guilty' to the Colonel. We'll both duck over into the Santa -'

"'Now, don't tell me what route you're going,' I interrupts,' 'cause I believe I'll stay and bluff it through, rather than sneak for it, though neither proposition don't appeal to me. I may get raised out before the draw, but the percentage is just as strong agin your game as mine.'

"'Boy, if I was backing your system,' says Kink, 'I'd shore copper this move and play her to lose. You come on with me, and we'll make it through - mebbe.'

"'No,' I says; 'here I sticks.'

"I made up a pack-strap out of my extry overhalls while he got grub together, to start south through one hundred miles of the ruggedest and barrenest country that was ever left unfinished.

"Next noon I was parching some coffee-beans in the frying-pan, when I heard hoofs down the gully back of me. I never looked up when they come into the open nor when I heard a feller say 'Halt!'

"'Hello there!' somebody yells. 'You there at the fire.' I kept on shaking the skillet over the camp-fire.

"'What's the matter with him?' somebody said. A man got off and walked up behind me.

"'See here, brother,' he says, tapping me on the

Rex E. Beach

shoulder; 'this don't go.'

"I jumped clean over the fire, dropped the pan, and let out a deaf and dumb holler, 'Ee! Ah!'

"The men began to laugh; it seemed to rile the little leftenant.

"'Cut this out,' says he. 'You can talk as well as I can, and you're a going to tell us about this Injun killin'. Don't try any fake business, or I'll roast your little heels over that fire like yams.'

"I just acted the dummy, wiggled my fingers, and handed him the joyful gaze, heliographing with my teeth as though I was glad to see visitors. However, I wondered if that runt would really give my chilblains a treat. He looked like a West Pointer, and I didn't know but he'd try to haze me.

"Well! they 'klow-towed' around there for an hour looking for clues, but I'd hid all the signs of Kink, so finally they strapped me onto a horse and we hit back for the fort.

"The little man tried all kinds of tricks to make me loosen on the way down, but I just acted wounded innocence and 'Ee'd' and 'Ah'd' at him till he let me alone.

"When we rode up to the post he says to the Colonel:

"'We've got the only man there is in the mountains back there, sir, but he's playing dumb. I don't know what his game is.'

"'Dumb, eh?' says the old man, looking me over pretty keen. 'Well! I guess we'll find his voice if he's got one.'

"He took me inside, and speaking of examinations, probably I didn't get one. He kept looking at me like he wanted to place me, but I give him the 'Ee! Ah!' till everybody began to laugh. They tried me with a pencil and paper, but I balked, laid my ears back, and buck-jumped. That made the old man sore, and he says: 'Lock him up! Lock him up; I'll make him talk if I have to skin him.' So I was dragged to the 'skookum-house,' where I spent the night figuring out my finish.

"I could feel it coming just as plain, and I begun to see that when I did open up and prattle after Kink was safe, nobody wouldn't believe my little story. I had sized the Colonel up as a dead stringy old proposition, too. He was one of these big-chopped fellers with a mouth set more'n half way up from his chin and little thin lips like the edge of a knife blade, and just as full of blood - face, big and rustic-finished.

"I says to myself, 'Bud, it looks like you wouldn't be forced to prospect for a living any more this season. If that old sport turns himself loose you're going to get 'life' three times and a holdover.'

"Next morning they tried every way to make me talk. Once in a while the old man looked at me puzzled and searching, but I didn't know him from a sweat-pad, and just paid strict attention to being dumb.

"It was mighty hard, too. I got so nervous my mouth simply ached to let out a cayoodle. The words kept trying to crawl through my sesophagus, and when I backed 'em up, they slid down and stood around in groups, hanging onto the straps, gradually filling me with witful gems of thought.

"The Colonel talked to me serious and quiet, like I had good ears, and says, 'My man, you can understand every word I say, I'm sure, and what your object is in maintaining this ridiculous silence, I don't know. You're accused of a crime, and it looks serious for you."

"Then he gazes at me queer and intent, and says, 'If you only knew how bad you are making your case you'd make a clean breast of it. Come now, let's get at the truth.'

"Them thought jewels and wads of repartee was piling up in me fast, like tailings from a ground-sluice, till I could feel myself getting bloated and pussy with langwidge, but I thought, 'No! to-morrow Kink 'll be safe, and then I'll throw a jolt into this man's camp that'll go down in history. They'll think some Chinaman's been thawing out a box of giant powder when I let out my roar.'

"I goes to the guard-house again, with a soldier at my back. Everything would have been all right if we hadn't run into a mule team.

"They had been freighting from the railroad, and as we left the barracks we ran afoul of four outfits, three span to the wagon, with the loads piled on till the teams was all lather and the wheels complainin' to the gods, trying to pass the corner of the barracks where there was a narrow opening between the buildings.

"Now a good mule-driver is the littlest, orneriest speck

in the human line that's known to the microscope, but when you get a poor one, he'd spoil one of them cholera germs you read about just by contact. The leader of this bunch was worse than the worst; strong on whip-arm, but surprising weak on judgment. He tried to make the turn, run plump into the corner of the building, stopped, backed, swung, and proceeded to get into grief.

"The mules being hot and nervous, he sent them all to the loco patch instanter. They began to plunge and turn and back and snarl. Before you could say 'Craps! you lose,' them shave-tails was giving the grandest exhibition of animal idiocy in the Territory, barring the teamster. He follered their trail to the madhouse, yanking the mouths out of them, cruel and vicious.

"Now, one mule can cause a heap of tribulation, and six mules can break a man's heart, but there wasn't no excuse for that driver to stand up on his hind legs, close his eyes, and throw thirty foot of lash into that plunging buckin', white-eyed mess. When he did it, all the little words inside of me began to foam and fizzle like sedlitz; out they came, biting, in mouthfuls, and streams, and squirts, backwards, sideways, and through my nose.

"'Here! you infernal half-spiled, dog-robbing walloper,' I says; 'you don't know enough to drive puddle ducks to a pond. You quit heaving that quirt or I'll harm you past healing.'

"He turned his head and grit out something through his teeth that stimulated my circulation. I skipped over the wheels and put my left onto his neck, fingering the keys on his blow-pipe like a flute. Then I give him a toss and gathered up the lines. Say! it was like the smell of grease-paint to an actor man for me to feel the ribbons again, and them mules knew they had a chairman who savvied 'em too, and had mule talk pat, from soda to hock.

"I just intimated things over them with that whip, and talked to them like they was my own flesh and blood. I starts at the worst words the English langwidge and the range had produced, to date, and got steadily and rapidly worse as long as I talked.

"Arizony may be slow in the matter of standing collars and rag-time, but she leads the world in profanity. Without being swelled on myself, I'll say, too, that I once had more'n a local reputation in that line, having originated some quaint and feeling conceits which has won modest attention, and this day I was certainly trained to the minute.

"I addressed them brutes fast and earnest for five minutes steady, and never crossed my trail or repeated a thought.

"It must have been sacred and beautiful. Anyhow, it was strong enough to soak into their pores so that they strung out straight as a chalk-line. Then I lifted them into the collars, and we rumbled past the building, swung in front of the commissary door, cramped and stopped. With the wheelers on their haunches, I backed up to the door square as a die.

"I wiped the sweat out of my eyes and looked up into the grinning face of about fifty swatties, realizing I was a mute - and a prisoner.

"I heard a voice say, 'Bring me that man.' There stood the Colonel oozing out wrath at every pore.

"I parted from that wagon hesitating and reluctant, but two soldiers to each leg will bust any man's grip, I lost some clothes, too, after we hit the ground, but I needed the exercise.

"The old man was alone in his office when they dragged me in, and he sent my guards out.

"'So you found your voice, did you?' he says.

"'Yes, sir," I answers. 'It came back unexpected, regular miracle.'

"'He drummed on the table for a long time, and then says, sort of immaterial and irreverent, 'You're a pretty good mule puncher, eh?'

"'It ain't for me to say I'm the best in the Territory,' I says; 'but I'm curious to meet the feller that claims the title.'

"He continues, 'It reminds me of an exhibition I saw once, back in New Mexico, long time ago, at the little Flatwater Canyon.'

"'Maybe you've heard tell of the fight there when the Apaches were up? Yes? Well, I happened to be in that scrimmage.'

"'I was detailed with ten men to convoy a wagon train through to Fort Lewis. We had no trouble till we came to the end of that canyon, just where she breaks out onto the flats. There we got it. They were hidden up on the ridges; we lost two men and one wagon before we could get out onto the prairie.

"'I got touched up in the neck, first clatter, and was bleeding pretty badly; still I hung to my horse, and we stood 'em off till the teams made it out of the gulch; but just as we came out my horse fell and threw me - broke his leg. I yelled to the boys:

"'"Go on! For God's sake go on!" Any delay there meant loss of the whole outfit. Besides, the boys had more than they could manage, Injuns on three sides.

"'We had a young Texan driving the last wagon. When I went down he swung those six mules of his and came back up that trail into the gut, where the bullets snapped like grasshoppers.

"'It was the prettiest bit of driving I ever saw, not to mention nerve. He whirled the outfit between me and the bluff on two wheels, yelling, "Climb on! Climb on! We ain't going to stay long!" I was just able to make it onto the seat. In the turn they dropped one of his wheelers. He ran out on the tongue and cut the brute loose. We went rattling down the gulch behind five mules. All the time there came out of that man's lungs the fiercest stream of profanity my ears ever burned under. I was pretty sick for a few weeks, so I never got a chance to thank that teamster. He certainly knew the mind of an army mule, though. His name was - let me see - Wiggins - yes, Wiggins.

"'Oh, no it wasn't,' I breaks in, foolish; 'it was Joyce.'

"Then I stopped and felt like a kid, for the Colonel comes up and shuts the circulation out of both my hands.

"'I wasn't sure of you, Bill,' he says, 'till I saw you preside over those mules out there and heard your speech - then I recognized the gift.' He laughed like a boy, still making free with my hands. 'I'm darn glad to see you, Bill Joyce. Now then,' he says, 'tell me all about this killing up in the hills,' and I done so.

"After I finished he never said anything for a long time, just drummed the desk again and looked thoughtful.

"'It's too bad you didn't speak out, Bill, when you first came in. Now, you've showed everybody that you can talk - just a little, anyhow,' and he smiles, 'and they all think you're the man caused the trouble. I don't see but that you've got to stand trial. I wish I could help you, Bill.'

"'But see here, Colonel,' I says; 'I couldn't squeal on Kink. We're *pardners*. I just *had* to give him a chance to cut. I played dumb 'cause I knew if I talked at all, being simple and guileless, you all would twist me up and have the whole thing in a jiffy. That man give me the last drop of water in his canteen on the Mojave, and him with his own tongue swelled clean out of his mouth, too. When we was snowed in, up in the Bitter Roots, with me snow-blind and starving, he crawled from Sheeps-Horn clean to Miller's - snow twelve foot deep, too, and nary a snow-shoe in miles, but he brought the outfit in to where I was lyin' 'bout gone in. He lost some fingers and more toes wallering through them mountain drifts that day, but he never laid down till he brought the boys back.

Rex E. Beach

"'Colonel! we've slept on the same blanket, we've et the same grub, we've made and lost together, and I had to give him a show, that's all. I'm into this here trouble now. Tell me how I'm going to get out. What would you do?'

"He turns to the open window and says: 'Partners are partners! That's my horse out there at that post. If I were you I'd run like hell.'

"That was the willingest horse I ever rode, and I hated to sell him, but he was tolable used up when I got across the line."

THE COLONEL AND THE HORSE-THIEF

Those marks on my arm? Oh! I got 'em playin' horse-thief. Yes, playin'. I wasn't a real one, you know - Well, I s'pose it was sort of a queer game. Came near bein' my last too, and if Black Hawk hadn't been the best horse in Texas the old Colonel would've killed me sure. He chased me six miles as it was - me with one arm full of his buckshot and anxious to explain, and him strainin' to get in range again and not wishin' any further particulars.

That was way back in the sixties, when I was as wild a lad as ever straddled a pony.

You see five of us had gone over into the Crow Nation to race horses with the Indians, and it was on the way back that the old man and the bullet holes figger in the story.

At the beginnin' it was Jim Barrett's plan, and it had jest enough risk and devilment in it to suit a harum-scarum young feller like me; so we got five of the boys who had good horses, lumped together all of our money, and rode out to invade the reservation.

You know how an Indian loves to run horses? Well, the Crows had a good deal of money then, and our scheme was to go over there, get up a big race, back our horses with all we had, and take down the wealth.

Takin' chances? Don't you believe it. That's where the beauty of Jim's plan commenced to sort of shine through.

You see, as soon as the money was up and the horses started, every Indian would be watchin' the race and yellin' at the nags, then, in the confusion, our boys was to grab the whole pot, Indian's money and ours too, and we'd make our get away across the river back into Texas.

We figured that we could get a few minutes start of 'em, and, with the horses we had under us, there wasn't much danger of their gettin' in range before we crossed back to where they couldn't follow us.

Well, sir! I never see anything work out like that scheme did. Them Crows was dead anxious to run their ponies and seemed skeered that we wouldn't let 'em get all their money up.

As we was eatin' supper the night before the race, Donnelly says: "Boys, I'm sore that we didn't have more coin. If we'd worked 'em right they'd 'a' give us odds. We could 'a' got five to three anyhow, and maybe more."

"They shore have got a heap of confidence in them skates of their'n," says Kink Martin. "I never see anybody so anxious to play a race in my life. If it wasn't all planned out the way it is, I'd like to stick and see which hoss is the best. I'd back Black Hawk agin any hunk of meat in the Territory, with the Kid here in the saddle."

They'd ribbed it up for me to ride Martin's mare, Black Hawk, while a little feller named Hollis rode his own horse.

Donnelly's part was to stay in the saddle and keep the other horses close to Barrett and Martin. They was to stick next to the money, and one of 'em do the bearin' off of the booty while the other made the protection play.

We hoped in the excitement to get off without harmin' any of Uncle Sam's pets, but all three of the boys had been with the Rangers and I knew if it came to a show down, they wouldn't hesitate to "pot" one or two in gittin' away.

We rode out from camp the next mornin' to where we'd staked out a mile track on the prairie and it seemed as if the whole Crow Nation was there, and nary a white but us five.

They'd entered two pretty good-lookin' horses and had their jockeys stripped down to breech-clouts, while Hollis and me wore our whole outfits on our backs, as we didn't exactly figger on dressin' after the race, leastways, not on that side of the river.

Just before we lined up, Jim says: "Now you - all ride like -, and when you git to the far turn we'll let the guns loose and stampede the crowd. Then jest leave the track and make a break fer the river, everybody fer himself. We'll all meet at them cottonwoods on the other side, so we can stand 'em off if they try to swim across after us."

That would have been a sure enough hot race if we had

run it out, for we all four got as pretty a start as I ever see and went down the line all together with a-bangin' of hoofs and Indian yells ringin' in our ears.

I had begun to work Black Hawk out of the bunch to get a clear start across the prairie at the turn, when I heard the guns begin snappin' like pop-corn.

"They've started already," yelled Hollis, and we turned the rearin' horses toward the river, three miles away, leavin' them two savages tearin' down the track like mad.

I glanced back as I turned, but, instead of seein' the boys in the midst of a decent retreat, the crowd was swarmin' after 'em like a nest of angry hornets, while Donnelly, with his reins between his teeth, was blazin' away at three reds who were right at Barrett's heels as he ran for his horse. Martin was lashin' his jumpin' cayuse away from the mob which sputtered and spit angry shots after him. Bucks were runnin' here and there and hastily mountin' their ponies - while an angry roar came to me, punctuated by the poppin' of the guns.

Hollis and I reached the river and swam it half a mile ahead of the others and their yellin' bunch of trailers, so we were able to protect 'em in their crossin'.

I could see from their actions that Bennett and Martin was both hurt and I judged the deal hadn't panned out exactly accordin' to specifications.

The Crows didn't attempt to cross in the teeth of our fire, however, being satisfied with what they'd done, and the horses safely brought our three comrades drippin' up the bank to where we lay takin' pot-shots at every bunch of feathers that approached the opposite bank.

We got Barrett's arm into a sling, and, as Martin's hurt wasn't serious, we lost no time in gettin' away.

"They simply beat us to it," complained Barrett, as we rode south. "You all had jest started when young Long Hair grabs the sack and ducks through the crowd, and the whole bunch turns loose on us at once. We wasn't expectin' anything so early in the game, and they winged me the first clatter. I thought sure it was oft with me when I got this bullet in the shoulder, but I used the gun in my left hand and broke for the nearest pony."

"They got me, too, before I saw what was up," added Martin; "but I tore out of there like a jack-rabbit. It was all done so cussed quick that the first thing I knew I'd straddled my horse and was makin' tracks. Who'd a thought them durned Indians was dishonest enough fer a trick like that?"

Then Donnelly spoke up and says: "Boys, as fur as the coin goes, we're out an' injured; we jest made a 'Mexican stand-off' - lost our money, but saved our lives - and mighty lucky at that, from appearances. What I want to know now is, how we're all goin' to get home, clean across the State of Texas, without a dollar in the outfit, and no assets but our guns and the nags."

That was a sure tough proposition, and we had left it teetotally out of calculations. We'd bet every bean on that race, not seein' how we could lose. In them days there wasn't a railroad in that section, ranches were scatterin', and people weren't givin' pink teas to every stranger that rode up - especially when they were as hard-lookin' as we were.

"We've got to eat, and so's the horses," says Hollis, "but no rancher is goin' to welcome with open arms as disreputable an outfit as we are. Two men shot up, and the rest of us without beddin', grub, money, or explanations. Them's what we need - explanations. I don't exactly see how we're goin' to explain our fix to the honest hay-diggers, either. Everybody'll think some sheriff is after us, and two to one they'll put some officer on our trail, and we'll have more trouble. I believe I've had all I want for awhile."

"I'll tell you how we'll work it," I says. "One of us'll be the sheriff of Guadalupe County, back home, with three deputies, bringin' back a prisoner that we've chased across the State. We'll ride up to a ranch an' demand lodgin' for ourselves and prisoner in the name of the State of Texas and say that we'll pay with vouchers on the county in the morning."

"No, sir! not fer me," says Martin. "I'm not goin' in fer forgery. It's all right to practice a little mild deception on our red brothers, as we figgered on doing, but I'm not goin' to try to flimflam the State of Texas. Our troubles 'd only be startin' if we began that game."

"Your plan's all right, Kid," says Bennett to me. "You be the terrible desperado that I'm bringin' home after a bloody fight, where you wounded Martin and me, and 'most escaped. You'll have ev'ry rancher's wife givin' you flowers and weepin' over your youth and kissin' you good-bye. In the mornin', when we're ready to go and I'm about to fix up the vouchers for our host, you break away and ride like the devil. We'll all tear off a few shots and foller in a hurry, leavin' the farmer hopin' that the villain is recaptured and the girls tearfully prayin' that the gallunt and misguided youth escapes."

It seemed to be about our only resort, as the country was full of bad men, and we were liable to get turned down cold if we didn't have some story, so we decided to try it on.

We rode up to a ranch 'bout dark, that night, me between the others, with my hands tied behind me, and Jim called the owner out.

"I want a night's lodgin' fer my deputies and our prisoner," he says. "I'm the sheriff of Guadalupe County, and I'll fix up the bill in the mornin'."

"Come in! Come in!" the feller says, callin' a man for the horses. "Glad to accommodate you. Who's your prisoner?"

"That's Texas Charlie that robbed the Bank of Euclid single-handed," answers Jim. "He give us a long run clean across the State, but we got him jest as he was settin' over into the Indian Territory. Fought like a tiger."

It worked fine. The feller, whose name was Morgan, give us a good layout for the night and a bully breakfast next morning.

That desperado game was simply great. The other fellers attended to the horses, and I jest sat around lookin' vicious, and had my grub brought to me, while the women acted sorrowful and fed me pie and watermelon pickles.

When we was ready to leave next morning, Jim says: "Now, Mr. Morgan, I'll fix up them vouchers with you," and givin' me the wink, I let out a yell, and jabbin' the spurs into Black Hawk, we cleared the fence and was off like a puff of dust, with the rest of 'em shootin' and screamin' after me like mad.

Say! It was lovely - and when the boys overtook me, out of sight of the house, Morgan would have been astonished to see the sheriff, his posse, and the terrible desperado doubled up in their saddles laughin' fit to bust.

Well, sir! we never had a hitch in the proceedings for five days, and I was gettin' to feel a sort of pride in my record as a bank-robber, forger, horse-thief, and murderer, accordin' to the way Bennett presented it. He certainly was the boss liar of the range.

He had a story framed up that painted me as the bloodiest young tough the Lone Star had ever produced, and it never failed to get me all the attention there was in the house.

One night we came to the best lookin' place we'd seen, and, in answer to Jim's summons, out walked an old man, followed by two of the prettiest girls I ever saw, who joined their father in invitin' us in.

"Glad to be of assistance to you, Mr. Sheriff," he said. "My name is Purdy, sir! Colonel Purdy, as you may have heard. In the Mexican War, special mention three times for distinguished conduct. These are my daughters, sir! Annabel and Marie." As we went in, he continued: "You say you had a hard time gettin' your prisoner? He looks young for a criminal. What's he wanted for?"

Somehow, when I saw those girls blushin' and bowin' behind their father, I didn't care to have my crimes made out any blacker'n necessary and I tried to give Jim the high-sign to let me off easy - just make it forgery or arson - but he was lookin' at the ladies, and evidently believin' in the strength of a good impression, he said: "Well, yes! He's young but they never was a old man with half his crimes. He's wanted for a good many things in different places, but I went after him for horse-stealin' and murder. Killed a rancher and his little daughter, then set fire to the house and ran off a bunch o' stock."

"Oh! Oh! How dreadful!" shuddered the girls, backin' off with horrified glances at me.

I tried to get near Jim to step on his foot, but the old man was glarin' at me somethin' awful.

"Come to observe him closely, he has a depraved face," says he. "He looks the thorough criminal in every feature, dead to every decent impulse, I s'pose."

I could have showed him a live impulse that would have surprised him about then.

In those days I was considered a pretty handsome feller too, and I knew I had Jim beat before the draw on looks, but he continues makin' matters worse.

"Yes, and he's desperate too. One of the worst I ever

see. We had an awful fight with him up here on the line of the Territory. He shot Martin and me before we got him. Ye see, I wanted to take him alive, and so I took chances on gettin' hurt.

"Thank ye, Miss; my arm does ache considerable; of course, if you'd jest as soon dress it - Oh, no! I'm no braver'n anybody else, I guess. Nice of ye to say so, anyhow," and he went grinnin' out into the kitchen with the girls to fix up his arm.

The old man insisted on havin' my feet bound together and me fastened to a chair, and said: "Yes, yes, I know you can watch him, but you're in my house now, and I feel a share of the responsibility upon me. I've had experience with desperate characters and I'm goin' to be sure that this young reprobate don't escape his just punishment. Are you sure you don't need more help gettin' him home? I'll go with you if - "

"Thank ye," interrupted Hollis. "We've chased the scoundrel four hundred miles, and I reckon, now we've got him, we can keep him."

At supper, Jim with his arm in a new sling, sat between the two girls who cooed over him and took turns feedin' him till it made me sick.

The old man had a nigger move my chair up to the foot of the table and bring me a plate of coarse grub after they all finished eatin'.

He had tied my ankles to the lower rung of the chair himself, and when I says to the nigger, "Those cords have plum stopped my circulation, just ease 'em up a little," he went straight up.

"Don't you touch them knots, Sam!" he roared. "I know how to secure a man, and don't you try any of your games in my house, either, you young fiend. I'd never forgive myself if you escaped."

I ate everything I could reach, which wasn't much, and when I asked for the butter he glared at me and said: "Butter's too good for horse-thieves; eat what's before you."

Every time I'd catch the eye of one of the girls and kind of grin and look enticing, she'd shiver and tell Jim that the marks of my depravity stood out on my face like warts on a toad.

Jim and the boys would all grin like idiots and invent a new crime for me. On the square, if I'd worked nights from the age of three I couldn't have done half they blamed me for.

They put it to the old man so strong that when he turned in he chained me to Sam, the cross-eyed nigger that stood behind me at supper, and made us sleep on the floor.

I told Sam that I cut a man's throat once because he snored, and that nigger never closed an eye all night. I was tryin' to get even with somebody.

After breakfast, when it came time to leave, Donnelly untied my feet and led me out into the yard, where the girls were hangin' around the Colonel and Jim, who was preparin' to settle up.

As we rode up the evening before, I had noticed that we turned in from the road through a lane, and that the fence was too high to jump, so, when I threw my leg over Black Hawk, I hit Donnelly a swat in the neck, and, as he did a stage-fall, I swept through the gate and down the lane.

The old man cut the halter off one of his Mexican war-whoops, and broke through the house on the run, appearin' at the front door with his shot-gun just as I checked up to make the turn onto the main road.

As I swung around, doubled over the horse's neck, he let drive with his old blunderbuss, and I caught two buckshot in my right arm where you see them marks.

I had sense enough to hang on and ride for my life, because I knew the old fire-eater would reckon it a pleasure to put an end to such a wretch as me, if he got half a chance.

I heard him howl, "Come on boys! We'll get him yet," and, over my shoulder, I saw him jump one of his loose horses standin' in the yard and come tearin' down the lane, ahead of the befuddled sheriff and posse, his white hair streamin' and the shot-gun wavin' aloft, as though chargin' an army of greasers at the head of his regiment.

From the way he drew away from the boys, I wouldn't have placed any money that he was wrong either.

I've always wondered how the old man ever got through that war with only three recommendations to the government.

He certainly kept good horses too, for in five minutes we'd left the posse behind, and I saw him madly urgin' his horse into range, reloadin' as he came.

As I threw the quirt into the mare with my good arm, I allowed I'd had about all the horse-stealin' I wanted for a while.

The old devil finally saw he was losin' ground in spite of his best efforts, and let me have both barrels. I heard the shot patter on the hard road behind me, and hoped he'd quit and go home, but I'm blamed if he didn't chase me five miles further before turnin' back, in hopes I'd cast a shoe or something would happen to me.

I believe I was on the only horse in Texas that could have outrun the Colonel and his that mornin'.

About noon I stopped at a blacksmith's shop, half dead with pain, and had my arm dressed and a big jolt of whiskey.

As the posse rode up to me, sittin' in the sun by the lathered flanks of my horse and nursin' my arm, Jim yells out: "Here he is! Surround him, boys! You're our prisoner!"

"No! I'm blamed if I am," I says. "You'll have to get another desperado. After this, I'm the sheriff!"

THE THAW AT SLISCO'S

The storm broke at Salmon Lake, and we ran for Slisco's road-house. It whipped out from the mountains, all tore into strips coming through the saw-teeth, lashing us off the glare ice and driving us up against the river banks among the willows. Cold? Well, some! My bottle of painkiller froze slushy, like lemon punch.

There's nothing like a warm shack, with a cache full of grub, when the peaks smoke and the black snow-clouds roar down the gulch.

Other "mushers" were ahead of us at the road-house, freighters from Kougarok, an outfit from Teller going after booze, the mail-carrier, and, who do you reckon? - Annie Black. First time I had seen her since she was run out of Dawson for claim jumping.

Her and me hadn't been essential to one another since I won that suit over a water right on Eldorado.

"Hello, Annie," says I, clawing the ice out of my whiskers; "finding plenty of claims down here to relocate?"

"Shut up, you perjured pup," says she, full of disappointing affabilities; "I don't want any dealings with a lying, thieving hypocrite like you, Billy Joyce."

Annie lacks the sporting instinct; she ain't got the disposition for cup-racing. Never knew her to win a case, and yet she's the instigatress of more emotional activities than all the marked cards and home distilled liquor in Alaska.

"See here," says I, "a prairie dog and a rattler can hole up together, but humans has got to be congenial, so, seein' as we're all stuck to live in the same room till this blizzard blizzes out, let's forget our troubles. I'm as game a Hibernian as the next, but I don't hibernate till there's a blaze of mutual respect going."

"Blaze away," says she, "though I leave it to the crowd if you don't look and act like a liar and a grave robber." Her speech is sure full of artless hostilities.

Ain't ever seen her? Lord! I thought everybody knew Annie Black. She drifted into camp one day, tall, slab-sided, ornery to the view, and raising fifty or upwards; disposition uncertain as frozen dynamite. Her ground plans and elevations looked like she was laid out for a man, but the specifications hadn't been follered. We ain't consumed by curiosity regarding the etymology of every stranger that drifts in, and as long as he totes his own pack, does his assessments, and writes his location notices proper, it goes. Leastways, it went till she hit town. In a month she had the brotherly love of that camp gritting its teeth and throwing back twisters. 'Twas all legitimate, too, and there never was a penny-weight of scandal connected with her name. No, sir! Far's conduct goes, she's always been the shinin' female example of this country; but them qualities let her out.

First move was to jump Bat Ruggles's town lot. He had four courses of logs laid for a cabin when "Scotty" Bell came in from the hills with $1800 in coarse gold that he'd rocked out of a prospect shaft on Bat's Moose's Creek claim.

Naturally Bat made general proclamation of thirst, and our town kinder dozed violently into a joyful three days' reverie, during which period of coma the recording time on Bat's lot ran out.

He returns from his "hootch-hunt" to complete the shack, and finds Annie overseeing some "Siwashes" put a pole roof on it. Of course he promotes a race-war immediate, playing the white "open" and the red to lose, so to speak, when she up an' spanks his face, addressing expurgated, motherly cuss-words at him like he'd been a bad boy and swallered his spoon, or dug an eye out of the kitten. Bat realizes he's against a strange system and draws out of the game.

A week later she jumps No. 3, Gold Bottom, because Donnelly stuck a pick in his foot and couldn't stay to finish the assessment.

"I can't throw her off, or shoot her up," says he, "or even cuss at her like I want to, 'cause she's a lady." And it appeared like that'd been her graft ever since - presumin' on her sex to make disturbances. In six months we hated her like pizen.

There wasn't a stampede in a hundred miles where her bloomers wasn't leading, for she had the endurance of a moose; and between excitements she prospected for trouble in the manner of relocations.

I've heard of fellers speakin' disrespectful to her and then wandering around dazed and loco after she'd got through painting word pictures of 'em. It goes without saying she was generally popular and petted, and when the Commissioner invited her to duck out down the river, the community sighed, turned over, and had a peaceful rest - first one since she'd come in.

I hadn't seen her from that time till I blowed into Slisco's on the bosom of this forty mile, forty below blizzard.

Setting around the fire that night I found that she'd just lost another of her famous lawsuits - claimed she owned a fraction 'longside of No. 20, Buster Creek, and that the Lund boys had changed their stakes so as to take in her ground. During the winter they'd opened up a hundred and fifty feet of awful rich pay right next to her line, and she'd raised the devil. Injunctions, hearings and appeals, and now she was coming back, swearing she'd been "jobbed," the judge had been bought, and the jury corrupted.

"It's the richest strike in the district," says she. "They've rocked out $11,000 since snow flew, and there's 30,000 buckets of dirt on the dump. They can bribe and bulldoze a decision through this court, but I'll have that fraction yet, the robbers."

"Robbers be cussed," speaks up the mail man. "You're the cause of the trouble yourself. If you don't get a square deal, it's your own fault - always looking for technicalities in the mining laws. It's been your game from the start to take advantage of your skirts, what there is of 'em, and jump, jump, jump. Nobody believes half you say. You're a natural disturber, and if you was a man you'd have been hung long ago."

I've heard her oral formations, and I looked for his epidermis to shrivel when she got her replications focused. She just soared up and busted.

"Look out for the stick," thinks I.

"Woman, am I," she says, musical as a bum gramophone under the slow bell. "I take advantage of my skirts, do I? Who are you, you mangy 'malamoot,' to criticise a lady? I'm more of a man than you, you tinhorn; I want no favours; I do a man's work; I live a man's life; I am a man, and I'm proud of it, but you -; Nome's full of your kind; you need a woman to support you; you're a protoplasm, a polyp. Those Swedes changed their stakes to cover my fraction. I know it, they know it, and if it wasn't Alaska, God would know it, but He won't be in again till spring, and then the season's only three months long. I've worked like a man, suffered like a man - "

"Why don't ye' lose like a man?" says he.

"I will, and I'll fight like one, too," says she, while her eyes burned like faggots. "They've torn away the reward of years of work and agony, and they forget I can hate like a man."

She was stretched up to high C, where her voice drowned the howl of the storm, and her seamed old face was a sight. I've seen mild, shrinky, mouse-shy women 'roused to hell's own fury, and I felt that night that here was a bad enemy for the Swedes of Buster Creek.

She stopped, listening.

"What's that? There's some one at the door."

"Nonsense," says one of the freighters. "You do so much knocking you can hear the echo."

"There's some one at that door," says she.

"If there was, they'd come in," says Joe.

"Couldn't be, this late in this storm," I adds.

She came from behind the stove, and we let her go to the door alone. Nobody ever seemed to do any favours for Annie Black.

"She'll be seein' things next," says Joe, winking. "What'd I tell you? For God's sake close it - you'll freeze us."

Annie opened the door, and was hid to the waist in a cloud of steam that rolled in out of the blackness. She peered out for a minute, stooped, and tugged at something in the dark. I was at her side in a jump, and we dragged him in, snow-covered and senseless.

"Quick - brandy," says she, slashing at his stiff "mukluks." "Joe, bring in a tub of snow." Her voice was steel sharp.

"Well, I'm danged," says the mail man. "It's only an Injun. You needn't go crazy like he was a white."

"Oh, you *fool*" says Annie. "Can't you see? Esquimaux don't travel alone. There's white men behind, and

God help them if we don't bring him to."

She knew more about rescustications than us, and we did what she said, till at last he came out of it, groaning - just plumb wore out and numb.

"Talk to him, Joe; you savvy their noise," says I.

The poor devil showed his excitement, dead as he was.

"There's two men on the big 'Cut-off,'" Joe translates. "Lost on the portage. There was only one robe between 'em, so they rolled up in it, and the boy came on in the dark. Says they can't last till morning."

"That lets them out," says the mail carrier. "Too bad we can't reach them to-night."

"What!" snaps Annie. "Reach 'em? Huh! I said you were a jellyfish. Hurry up and get your things on, boys."

"Have a little sense," says Joe. "You surely ain't a darn fool. Out in this storm, dark as the inside of a cow; blowin' forty mile, and the 'quick' froze. Can't be done. I wonder who they are?"

He "kowtowed" some more, and at the answer of the chattering savage we looked at Annie.

"Him called Lund," shivered the Siwash.

I never see anybody harder hit than her. I love a scrap, but I thinks "Billy, she's having a stiffer fight than you ever associated with."

Finally she says, kind of slow and quiet: "Who knows where the 'Cut-off' starts?"

Nobody answers, and up speaks the U. S. man again.

"You've got your nerve, to ask a man out on such a night."

"If there was one here, I wouldn't have to ask him. There's people freezing within five miles of here, and you hug the stove, saying: 'It's stormy, and we'll get cold.' Of course it is. If it wasn't stormy they'd be here too, and it's so cold, you'll probably freeze. What's that got to do with it? Ever have your mother talk to you about duty? Thank Heaven I travelled that portage once, and I can find it again if somebody will go with me."

'Twas a blush raising talk, but nobody upset any furniture getting dressed.

She continues:

"So I'm the woman of this crowd and I hide behind my skirts. Mr. Mail Man, show what a glorious creature you are. Throw yourself - get up and stretch and roar. Oh, you barn-yard bantam! Has it had its pap to-night? I've a grand commercial enterprise; I'll take all of your bust measurements and send out to the States for a line of corsets. Ain't there half a man among you?"

She continued in this vein, pollutin' the air, and, having no means of defence, we found ourselves follerin' her out into a yelling storm that beat and roared over us like waves of flame.

Swede luck had guided their shaft onto the richest pay-streak in seven districts, and Swede luck now led us to the Lund boys, curled up in the drifted snow beside their dogs; but it was the level head and cool judgment of a woman that steered us home in the grey whirl of the dawn.

During the deathly weariness of that night I saw past the calloused hide of that woman and sighted the splendid courage cached away beneath her bitter oratory and hosstyle syllogisms. "There's a story there," thinks I, "an' maybe a man moved in it - though I can't imagine her softened by much affection." It pleased some guy to state that woman's the cause of all our troubles, but I figger they're like whisky - all good, though some a heap better'n others, of course, and when a frail, little, ninety pound woman gets to bucking and acting bad, there's generally a two hundred pound man hid out in the brush that put the burr under the saddle.

During the next three days she dressed the wounds of them Scow-weegians and nursed them as tender as a mother.

The wind hadn't died away till along came the "Flying Dutchman" from Dugan's, twenty miles up, floatin' on the skirts of the blizzard.

"Hello, fellers. Howdy, Annie. What's the matter here?" says he. "We had a woman at Dugan's too - purty as a picture; different from the Nome bunch - real sort of a lady."

"Who is she?" says I, "an' what's she doin' out here on the trail?"

"Dunno, but she's all right; come clean from Dawson with a dog team; says she's looking for her mother."

I heard a pan clatter on the floor where Annie was washing dishes, and her face went a sickly grey. She leaned across, gripping the table and straining to ask something, but the words wouldn't come, while "Dutch" continues:

"Somethin' strange about it, I think. She says her ma's over in the Golden Gate district, workin' a rich mine. Of course we all laughed at her, and said there wasn't a woman in the whole layout, 'ceptin' *some* folks might misconstrue Annie here into a kind of a female. She stuck to it though, much as to say we was liars. She's comin' on - what's the matter, Annie - you ain't sore at me effeminatin' you by the gentle name of female, are you?"

She had come to him, and gripped his shoulder, till her long, bony fingers buried themselves in his mackinaw. Her mouth was twitching, and she hadn't got shed of that "first-aid-to-the-injured" look.

"What name? What name, Dutch? What name?" She shook him like a rat.

"Bradshaw - but you needn't run your nails through and clinch 'em. Ow! Le'go my white meat. You act like she was your long lost baby. What d'ye think of that idea, fellers? Ain't that a pleasin' conceit? Annie Black, and a baby. Ha! Ha! that's a hit. Annie and a daughter. A cow-thief and a calla-lily."

"Dutch," says I, "you ain't a-goin' to make it through to Lane's Landing if you don't pull your freight," and I drags the darn fool out and starts him off.

When I came in she was huddled onto a goods box, shaking and sobbing like any woman, while the boys sat around and champed their bits and stomped.

"Take me away, Billy," she says. "For God's sake take me away before she sees me." She slid down to the floor and cried something awful. Gents, that was sure the real distress, nothing soft and sloppy, but hard, wrenchy, deep ones, like you hear at a melodrayma. 'Twas only back in '99 that I seen an awful crying match, though both of the ladies had been drinking, so I felt like I was useder to emotion than the balance of the boys, and it was up to me to take a holt.

"Madam," says I, and somehow the word didn't seem out of place any more - "Madam, why do you want to avoid this party?"

"Take me away," she says. "It's my daughter. She's going to find me this way, all rough and immodest and made fun of. But that's the worst you can say, isn't it? I'm a square woman - you know I am, don't you, boys?" and she looked at us fierce and pleadin'.

"Sure," says Joe. "We'll boost you with the girl all right."

"She thinks her father's dead, but he isn't - he ran away with a show woman - a year after we were married. I never told her about it, and I've tried to make a little lady of her."

We found out afterwards that she had put the girl in a boarding-school, but couldn't seem to make enough for both of them, and when the Klondyke was struck thought she saw a chance. She came north, insulted by deck hands and laughed at by the officers. At Skagway she nursed a man through typhoid, and when he could walk he robbed her. The mounted police took everything else she had and mocked at her. "Your kind always has money," they said.

That's how it had been everywhere, and that's why she was so hard and bitter. She'd worked and fought like a man, but she'd suffered like a woman.

"I've lied and starved and stolen for her," said Annie, "to make her think I was doing well. She said she was coming in to me, but I knew winter would catch her at Dawson, and I thought I could head her off by spring."

"Now, she's here; but, men, as your mothers loved you, save me from my little girl."

She buried her face, and when I looked at the boys, tears stood in Joe Slisco's eyes and the others breathed hard. Ole Lund, him that was froze worst about the hands, spoke up:

"Someboady tak de corner dat blanket an' blow may nose."

Then we heard voices outside.

"Hello, in there."

Annie stood up, clutching at her throat, and stepped behind the corner of the bunks as the door opened, framing the prettiest picture this old range rider ever saw.

'Twas a girl, glowing pink and red where the cold had kissed her cheeks, with yellow curlicues of hair wandering out under her yarn cap. Her little fox-trimmed parka quit at the knees, showing the daintiest pair of - I can't say it. Anyhow, they wasn't, they just looked like 'em, only nicer.

She stood blinking at us, coming from the bright light outside, as cute as a new faro box - then:

"Can you tell me where Mrs. Bradshaw lives? She's somewhere in this district. I'm her daughter - come all the way from the States to see her."

When she smiled I could hear the heart-strings of those ragged, whiskered, frost-bit "mushers" bustin' like banjo strings.

"You know her, don't you?" she says, turning to me.

"Know her, Miss? Well, I should snort! There ain't a prospector on the range that ain't proud and honoured to call her a friend. Leastways, if there is I'll bust his block," and I cast the bad eye on the boys to wise 'em up.

"Ain't I right, Joe?"

"Betcher dam life," says Joe, sort of over-stepping the conventions.

"Then tell me where her claim is. It's quite rich, and you must know it," says she, appealing to him.

Up against it? Say! I seen the whites of his eyes show like he was drownding, and he grinned joyful as a man kicked in the stummick.

"Er - er - I just bought in here, and ain't acquainted much," says he. "Have a drink," and, in his confusions, he sets out the bottle of alkalies that he dignifies by the alias of booze. Then he continues with reg'lar human intelligence.

"Bill, here, he can tell you where the ground is," and the whelp indicates me.

Lord knows my finish, but for Ole Lund. He sits up in his bunk, swaddled in Annie Black's bandages, and through slits between his frost bites, he moults the follering rhetoric:

"Aye tole you vere de claim iss. She own de Nomber Twenty fraction on Buster Creek, 'longside may and may broder. She's dam good fraction, too."

I consider that a blamed white stunt for Swedes; paying for their lives with the mine they swindled her out of.

Anyhow, it knocked us galley-west.

I'd formulated a swell climax, involving the discovery of the mother, when the mail man spoke up, him that had been her particular abomination, a queer kind of a break in his voice:

"Come out of that."

Mrs. Bradshaw moved out into the light, and, if I'm any judge, the joy that showed in her face rubbed away the bitterness of the past years. With an aching little cry the girl ran to her, and hid in her arms like a quail.

We men-folks got accumulated up into a dark corner where we shook hands and swore soft and insincere, and let our throats hurt, for all the world like it was Christmas or we'd got mail from home.

BITTER ROOT BILLINGS, ARBITER

Billings rode in from the Junction about dusk, and ate his supper in silence. He'd been East for sixty days, and, although there lurked about him the hint of unwonted ventures, etiquette forbade its mention. You see, in our country, that which a man gives voluntarily is ofttimes later dissected in smoky bunk-houses, or roughly handled round flickering camp fires, but the privacies he guards are inviolate. Curiosity isn't exactly a lost art, but its practice isn't popular nor hygenic.

Later, I found him meditatively whittling out on the porch, and, as the moment seemed propitious, I inquired adroitly: - "Did you have a good time in Chicago, 'Bitter Root'?"

"Bully," said he, relapsing into weighty absorption.

"What'd you do?" I inquired with almost the certainty of appearing insistent.

"Don't you never read the papers?" he inquired, with such evident compassion that Kink Martin and the other boys snickered. This from "Bitter Root," who scorns literature outside of the "Arkansas Printing," as he terms the illustrations!

"Guess I'll have to show you my press notices," and

from a hip pocket he produced a fat bundle of clippings in a rubber band. These he displayed jealously, and I stared agape, for they were front pages of great metropolitan dailies, marred with red and black scare heads, in which I glimpsed the words, "Billings, of Montana," "'Bitter Root' on Arbitration," "A Lochinvar Out of the West," and other things as puzzling.

"Press Notices!" echoed Kink scornfully. "Wouldn't that rope ye? He talks like Big Ike that went with the Wild West Show. When a puncher gets so lazy he can't earn a livin' by the sweat of his pony, he grows his hair, goes on the stage bustin' glass balls with shot ca'tridges and talks about 'press notices.' Let's see 'em, Billings. You pinch 'em as close to your stummick as though you held cards in a strange poker game."

"Well, I *have* set in a strange game, amongst aliens," said Billings, disregarding the request, "and I've held the high cards, also I've drawed out with honours. I've sailed the medium high seas with mutiny in the stoke-hold; I've changed the laws of labour, politics and municipal economies. I went out of God's country right into the heart of the decayin' East, and by the application of a runnin' noose in a hemp rope I strangled oppression and put eight thousand men to work." He paused ponderously. "I'm an Arbitrator!"

"The deuce you are," indignantly cried "Reddy" the cook. "Who says so?"

"Reddy" isn't up in syntax, and his unreasoning loyalty to Billings is an established fact of such standing that his remarks afford no conjecture.

"Yes, I've cut into the 'Nation's Peril' and the 'Cryin' Evil' good and strong - walkin' out from the stinks of the Union Stock Yards, of Chicago, into the limelight of publicity, via the 'drunk and disorderly' route.

"You see I got those ten carloads of steers into the city all right, but I was so blame busy splatterin' through the tracked-up wastes of the cow pens, an' inhalin' the sewer gas of the west side that I never got to see a newspaper. If I'd 'a' read one, here's what I'd 'a' found, namely: The greatest, stubbornest, riotin'est strike ever known, which means a heap for Chicago, she being the wet-nurse of labour trouble.

"The whole river front was tied up. Nary a steamer had whistled inside the six-mile crib for two weeks, and eight thousand men was out. There was hold-ups and blood-sheddin' and picketin', which last is an alias for assault with intents, and altogether it was a prime place for a cowman, on a quiet vacation - just homelike and natural.

"It was at this point that I enters, bustin' out of the smoke of the Stock Yards, all sweet and beautiful, like the gentle heeroine in the play as she walks through the curtains at the back of the stage.

"Now you know there's a heap of difference between the Stock Yards and Chicago - it's just like coming from Arkansas over into the United States.

"Well, soon as I sold the stock I hit for the lake front and began to ground sluice the coal dust off of my palate.

"I was busy working my booze hydraulic when I see an

Rex E. Beach

arid appearin' pilgrim 'longside lookin' thirsty as an alkali flat.

"'Get in,' says I, and the way he obeyed orders looked like he'd had military training. I felt sort of drawed to him from the way he handled his licker; took it straight and runnin' over; then sopped his hands on the bar and smelled of his fingers. He seemed to just soak it up both ways - reg'lar human blotter.

"'You lap it up like a man,' says I, 'like a cowman - full growed - ever been West?'

"'Nope,' says he, 'born here.'

"'Well I'm a stranger,' says I, 'out absorbin' such beauties of architecture and free lunch as offers along the line. If I ain't keepin' you up, I'd be glad of your company.'

"'I'm your assistant lunch buster,' says he, and in the course of things he further explained that he was a tugboat fireman, out on a strike, givin' me the follerin' information about the tie-up: -

"It all come up over a dose of dyspepsia -"

"Back up," interrupted Kink squirming, "are you plumb bug? Get together! You're certainly the Raving Kid. Ye must have stone bruised your heel and got concession of the brain."

"Yes sir! Indigestion," Billings continued. "Old man Badrich, of the Badrich Transportation Company has it terrible. It lands on his solar every morning about nine o'clock, gettin' worse steady, and reaches perihelion along about eleven. He can tell the time of day by taste. One morning when his mouth felt like about ten-forty-five in comes a committee from Firemen & Engineers Local No. 21, with a demand for more wages, proddin' him with the intimations that if he didn't ante they'd tie up all his boats."

"I 'spose a teaspoonful of bakin' soda, assimilated internally around the environments of his appendix would have spared the strike and cheated me out of bein' a hero. As the poet might have said - 'Upon such slender pegs is this, our greatness hung.'"

"Oh, Gawd!" exclaimed Mulling, piously.

"Anyhow, the bitterness in the old man's inner tubes showed in the bile of his answer, and he told 'em if they wanted more money he'd give 'em a chance to earn it - they could work nights as well as days. He intimated further that they'd ought to be satisfied with their wages as they'd undoubtedly foller the same line of business in the next world, and wouldn't get a cent for feedin' the fires neither.

"Next mornin' the strike was called, and the guy that breathed treachery and walk-outs was one 'Oily' Heegan, further submerged under the titles of President of the Federation of Fresh Water Firemen; also Chairman of the United Water-front Workmen, which last takes in everything doin' business along the river except the wharf-rats and typhoid germs, and it's with the disreputableness of this party that I infected myself to the detriment of labour and the triumph of the law.

"D. O'Hara Heegan is an able man, and inside of a week he'd spread the strike 'till it was the cleanest, dirtiest tie-up ever known. The hospitals and morgues was full of non-union men, but the river was empty all right. Yes, he had a persuadin' method of arbitration quite convincing to the most calloused, involving the layin' on of the lead pipe.

"Things got to be pretty fierce bye-and-bye, for they had the police buffaloed, and disturbances got plentyer than the casualties at a butchers' picnic. The strikers got hungry, too, finally, because the principles of unionism is like a rash on your mechanic, skin deep - inside, his gastrics works three shifts a day even if his outsides is idle and steaming with Socialism.

"Oily fed 'em dray loads of eloquence, but it didn't seem to be real fillin'. They'd leave the lectures and rob a bakery.

"He was a wonder though; just sat in his office, and kept the ship owners waitin' in line, swearin' bitter and refined cuss-words about 'ignorant fiend' and 'cussed pedagogue,' which last, for Kink's enlightenment, means a kind of Hebrew meetin'-house.

"These here details my new friend give me, ending with a eulogy on Oily Heegan, the Idol of the Idle.

"'If he says starve, we starve,' says he, 'and if he says work, we work. See! Oh he's the goods, he is! Let's go down by the river - mebbe we'll see him.' So me and Murdock hiked down Water Street, where they keep mosquito netting over the bar fixtures and spit at the stove.

"We found him, a big mouthed, shifty, kind of man, 'bout as cynical lookin' in the face as a black bass, and full of wind as a toad fish. I exchanged drinks for principles of socialism, and doin' so happened to display my roll. Murdock slipped away and made talk with a friend, then, when Heegan had left, he steers me out the back way into an alley. 'Short cut,' says he 'to another and a better place.'

"I follers through a back room; then as I steps out the door I'm grabbed by this new friend, while Murdock bathes my head with a gas-pipe billy, one of the regulation, strike promotin' kind, like they use for decoyin' members into the glorious ranks of Labour.

"I saw a 'Burning of Rome' that was a dream, and whole cloudbursts of shootin' stars, but I yanked Mr. Enthusiastic Stranger away from my surcingle and throwed him agin the wall. In the shuffle Murdock shifts my ballasts though, and steams up the alley with my greenbacks, convoyed by his friend.

"'Wow-ow,' says I, givin' the distress signal so that the windows rattled, and reachin' for my holster. I'd 'a' got them both, only the gun caught in my suspender. You see, not anticipatin' any live bird shoot I'd put it inside my pants-band, under my vest, for appearances. A forty-five is like fresh air to a drownding man - generally has to be drawed in haste - and neither one shouldn't be mislaid. I got her out at last and blazed away, just a second after they dodged around the comer. Then I hit the trail after 'em, lettin' go a few sky-shots and gettin' a ghost-dance holler off my stummick that had been troubling me. The wallop on the head made me dizzy though, and I zigzagged awful, tackin' out of the alley right into a policeman.

"'Whee!' says I in joy, for he had Murdock safe by the

bits, buckin' considerable.

"'Stan' aside and le'mme 'lectrocute 'im,' says I. I throwed the gun on him and the crowd dogged it into all the doorways and windows convenient, but I was so weak-minded in the knees I stumbled over the curb and fell down.

"Next thing I knew we was all bouncin' over the cobble-stones in a patrol wagon.

"Well, in the morning I told my story to the Judge, plain and unvarnished. Then Murdock takes the stand and busts into song, claiming that he was comin' through the alley toward Clark Street when I staggered out back of a saloon and commenced to shoot at him. He saw I was drunk, and fanned out, me shootin' at him with every jump. He had proof, he said, and he called for the president of his Union, Mr. Heegan. At the name all the loafers and stew-bums in the court-room stomped and said, 'Hear, hear,' while up steps this Napoleon of the Hoboes.

"Sure, he knew Mr. Murdock - had known him for years, and he was perfectly reliable and honest. As to his robbing me, it was preposterous, because he himself was at the other end of the alley and saw the whole thing, just as Mr. Murdock related it.

"I jumps up. 'You're a liar, Heegan. I was buyin' booze for the two of you;' but a policeman nailed me, chokin' off my rhetorics. Mr. Heegan leans over and whispers to the Judge, while I got chilblains along my spine.

"'Look here, kind Judge,' says I real winning and genteel, 'this man is so good at explainin' things away, ask him to talk off this bump over my ear. I surely didn't get a buggy spoke and laminate myself on the nut.

"'That'll do,' says the Judge. 'Mr. Clerk, ten dollars and costs - charge, drunk and disorderly. Next!'

"'Hold on there,' says I, ignorant of the involutions of justice, 'I guess I've got the bulge on you this time. They beat you to me, Judge. I ain't got a cent. You can go through me and be welcome to half you find. I'll mail you ten when I get home though, honest.'

"At that the audience giggled, and the Judge says: -

"'Your humour doesn't appeal to me, Billings. Of course, you have the privilege of working it out.' Oh, Glory, the 'Privilege!'

"Heegan nodded at this, and I realized what I was against.

"'Your honour,' says I with sarcastic refinements, 'science tells us that a perfect vacuum ain't possible, but after watching you I know better, and for you, Mr. Workingman's Friend, - us to the floor,' and I run at Heegan.

"Pshaw! I never got started, nor I didn't rightfully come to till I rested in the workhouse, which last figger of speech is a pure and beautiful paradox.

"I ain't dwellin' with glee on the next twenty-six days - ten dollars and costs, at four bits a day, but I left there saturated with such hatreds for Heegan that my breath smelted of 'em.

"I wanders down the river front, hoping the fortunes of war would deliver him to me dead or alive, when the thought hit me that I'd need money. It was bound to take another ten and costs shortly after we met, and probably more, if I paid for what I got, for I figgered on distendin' myself with satisfaction and his features with uppercuts. Then I see a sign, 'Non-Union men wanted - Big wages.' In I goes, and strains my lang-widge through a wire net at the cashier.

"'I want them big wages,' says I.

"'What can you do?'

"'Anything to get the money,' says I. 'What does it take to liquidate an assault on a labour leader?'

"There was a white-haired man in the cage who began to sit up and take notice.

"'What's your trouble?' says he, and I told him.

"'If we had a few more like you, we'd bust the strike,' says he, kind of sizin' me up. 'I've got a notion to try it anyhow,' and he smites the desk. 'Collins what d'ye say if we tow the "Detroit" out? Her crew has stayed with us so far, and they'll stick now if we'll say the word. The unions are hungry and scrapping among them-selves, and the men want to go back to work. It's just that devil of a Heegan that holds 'em. If they see we've got a tug crew that'll go, they'll arbitrate, and we'll kill the strike.'

"'Yes, sir!' says Collins, 'but where's the tug crew, Mr. Badrich?'"

"'Right here! We three, and Murphy, the bookkeeper. Blast this idleness! I want to fight.'

"'I'll take the same,' says I, 'when I get the price.'

"'That's all right. You've put the spirit into me, and I'll see you through. Can you run an engine? Good! I'll take the wheel, and the others'll fire. It's going to be risky work, though. You won't back out, eh?'"

Reddy interrupted Billings here loudly, with a snort of disgust, while "Bitter Root" ran his fingers through his hair before continuing. Martin was listening intently.

"The old man arranged to have a squad of cops on all the bridges, and I begin anticipatin' hilarities for next day.

"The news got out of course, through the secrecies of police headquarters, and when we ran up the river for our tow, it looked like every striker west of Pittsburg had his family on the docks to see the barbecue, accompanied by enough cobble-stones and scrap iron to ballast a battleship. All we got goin' up was repartee, but I figgered we'd need armour gettin' back.

"We passed a hawser to the 'Detroit,' and I turned the gas into the tug, blowin' for the Wells Street Bridge. Then war began. I leans out the door just in time to see the mob charge the bridge. The cops clubbed 'em back, while a roar went up from the docks and roof tops that was like a bad dream. I couldn't see her move none though, and old man Badrich blowed again expurgatin' himself of as nobby a line of cuss words as you'll muster outside the cattle belt.

"'Soak 'em,' I yells, 'give 'em all the arbitration you've got handy. If she don't open; we'll jump her,' and I lets out another notch, so that we went plowin' and boilin' towards the draw.

"It looked like we'd have to hurdle it sure enough, but the police beat the crowd back just in time. She wasn't clear open though, and our barge caromed off the spiles. It was like a nigger buttin' a persimmon tree - we rattled off a shower of missiles like an abnormal hail storm. Talk about your coast defence; they heaved everything at us from bad names to railroad iron, and we lost all our window glass the first clatter, while the smoke stack looked like a pretzel with cramps.

"When we scraped through I looked back with pity at the 'Detroit's' crew. She hadn't any wheel house, and the helmsman was due to get all the attention that was comin' to him. They'd built up a barricade of potato sacks, chicken coops and bic-a-brac around the wheel that protected 'em somewhat, but even while I watched, some Polack filtered a brick through and laid out the quartermaster cold, and he was drug off. Oh! it was refined and esthetic.

"Well, we run the gauntlet, presented every block with stuff rangin' in tensile strength from insults to asphalt pavements, and noise! - say, all the racket in the world was a whisper. I caught a glimpse of the old man leanin' out of the pilot house, where a window had been, his white hair bristly, and his nostrils h'isted, embellishin' the air with surprisin' flights of gleeful profanity.

"'Hooray! this is livin' he yells, spyin' me shovelin' the deck out from under the junk. 'Best scrap I've had in years,' and just then some baseball player throwed in from centre field, catching him in the neck with a tomato. Gee! that man's an honour to the faculty of speech.

"I was doin' bully till a cobble-stone bounced into the engine room, makin' a billiard with my off knee, then I got kind of peevish.

"Rush Street Bridge is the last one, and they'd massed there on both sides, like fleas on a razorback. Thinks I, 'If we make it through here, we've busted the strike,' and I glances back at the 'Detroit' just in time to see her crew pullin' their captain into the deck house, limp and bleedin'. The barricade was all knocked to pieces and they'd flunked absolute. Don't blame 'em much either, as it was sure death to stand out in the open under the rain of stuff that come from the bridges. Of course with no steerin' she commenced to swing off.

"I jumps out the far side of the engine room and yells fit to bust my throat.

"'Grab that wheel! Grab it quick - we'll hit the bridge,' but it was like deef and dumb talk in a boiler shop, while a wilder howl went up from the water front as they seen what they'd done and smelled victory. There's an awfulness about the voice of a blood-maddened club-swingin' mob; it lifts your scalp like a fright wig, particularly if you are the clubee.

"'We've got one chance,' thinks I, 'but if she strikes we're gone. They'll swamp us sure, and all the police in Cook County won't save enough for to hold services on.' Then I throwed a look at the opening ahead and the pessimisms froze in me.

"I forgot all about the resiliency of brickbats and the table manners of riots, for there, on top of a bunch of spiles, ca'm, masterful and bloated with perjuries, was Oily Heegan dictatin' the disposition of his forces, the light of victory in his shifty, little eyes.

"'Ten dollars and costs,' I shrieks, seein' red. 'Lemme crawl up them spiles to you.'

"Then inspiration seized me. My soul riz up and grappled with the crisis, for right under my mit, coiled, suggestive and pleadin', was one of the tug's heavin' lines, 'bout a three-eighths size. I slips a runnin' knot in the end and divides the coils, crouchin' behind the deck-house till we come abeam of him, then I straightened, give it a swinging heave, and the noose sailed up and settled over him fine and daisy.

"I jerked back, and Oily Heegan did a high dive from Rush Street that was a geometrical joy. He hit kind of amateurish, doin' what we used to call a 'belly-buster' back home, but quite satisfyin' for a maiden effort, and I reeled him in astern.

"Your Chicago man ain't a gamey fish. He come up tame and squirting sewage like a dissolute porpoise, while I played him out where he'd get the thrash of the propeller.

"'Help,' he yells, 'I'm a drownding.'

"'Ten dollars and costs," says I, lettin' him under again. 'Do you know who you're drinkin' with this time, hey?'

"I reckon the astonishment of the mob was equal to Heegan's; anyhow I'm told that we was favoured with such quietness that my voice sounded four blocks, simply achin' with satisfactions. Then pandemonium tore loose, but I was so engrosed in sweet converse I never heard it or noticed that the 'Detroit' had slid through the draw by a hair, and we was bound for the blue and smilin' lake.

"'For God's sake, lemme up,' says Heegan, splashin' along and look-in' strangly. I hauls him in where he wouldn't miss any of my ironies, and says: -

"'I just can't do it, Oily - it's wash day. You're plumb nasty with boycotts and picketin's and compulsory arbitrations. I'm goin' to clean you up,' and I sozzled him under like a wet shirt.

"I drug him out again and continues: -

"'This is Chinamen's work, Oily, but I lost my pride in the Bridewell, thanks to you. It's tough on St. Louis to laundry you up stream this way, but maybe the worst of your heresies 'll be purified when they get that far.' You know the Chicago River runs up hill out of Lake Michigan through the drainage canal and into the St. Louis waterworks. Sure it does - most unnatural stream I ever see about direction and smells.

"I was gettin' a good deal of enjoyment and infections out of him when old man Badrich ran back enamelled with blood and passe tomato juice, the red in his white hair makin' his top look like one of these fancy ice-cream drinks you get at a soda fountain.

"'Here! here! you'll kill him,' says he, so I hauled him aboard, drippin' and clingy, wringin' him out good and thorough - by the neck. He made a fine mop.

"These clippings," continued "Bitter Root," fishing into his pocket, "tell in beautiful figgers how the last seen of Oily Heegan he was holystoning the deck of a sooty little tugboat under the admonishments and feet of 'Bitter Root' Billings of Montana, and they state how the strikers tried to get tugs for pursuit and couldn't, and how, all day long, from the housetops was visible a tugboat madly cruisin' about inside the outer cribs, bustin' the silence with joyful blasts of victory, and they'll further state that about dark she steamed up the river, tired and draggled, with a bony-lookin' cowboy inhalin' cigareets on the stern-bits, holding a three-foot knotted rope in his lap. When a delegation of strikers met her, inquirin' about one D. O'Hara Heegan, it says like this," and Billings read laboriously as follows: -

"'Then the bronzed and lanky man arose with a smile of rare contentment, threw overboard his cigarette, and approaching the boiler-room hatch, called loudly: "Come out of that," and the President of the Federation of Fresh Water Firemen dragged himself wearily out into the flickering lights. He was black and drenched and streaked with sweat; also, he shone with the grease and oils of the engines, while the palms of his hands were covered with painful blisters from unwonted, intimate contact with shovels and drawbars. It was seen that he winced fearfully as the cowboy twirled the rope end.

"'"He's got the makin's of a fair fireman,"' said the stranger, "'all he wants is practice.'"

"Then, as the delegation murmured angrily, he held up his hand and, in the ensuing silence, said: -

"'"Boys, the strike's over. Mr. Heegan has arbitrated."'"

THE SHYNESS OF SHORTY

Bailey smoked morosely as he scanned the dusty trail leading down across the "bottom" and away over the dry grey prairie toward the hazy mountains in the west.

From his back-tilted chair on the veranda, the road was visible for miles, as well as the river trail from the south, sneaking up through the cottonwoods and leprous sycamores.

He called gruffly into the silence of the house, and his speech held the surliness of his attitude.

"Hot Joy! Bar X outfit comin'. Git supper."

A Chinaman appeared in the door and gazed at the six-mule team descending the distant gully to the ford.

"Jesse one man, hey? All light," and slid quietly back to the kitchen.

Whatever might be said, or, rather, whatever might be suspected, of Bailey's road-house - for people did not run to wordy conjecture in this country - it was known that it boasted a good cook, and this atoned for a catalogue of shortcomings. So it waxed popular among the hands of the big cattle ranges near-bye. Those given to idle talk held that Bailey acted strangely at times, and rumour painted occasional black doings at the hacienda, squatting vulture-like above the ford, but it was nobody's business, and he kept a good cook.

Bailey did not recall the face that greeted him from above the three span as they swung in front of his corral, but the brand on their flanks was the Bar X, so he nodded with as near an approach to hospitality as he permitted.

It was a large face, strong-featured and rugged, balanced on wide, square shoulders, yet some oddness of posture held the gaze of the other till the stranger clambered over the wheel to the ground. Then Bailey removed his brier and heaved tempestuously in the throes of great and silent mirth.

It was a dwarf. The head of a Titan, the body of a whisky barrel, rolling ludicrously on the tiny limbs of a bug, presented so startling a sight that even Hot Joy, appearing around the corner, cackled shrilly. His laughter rose to a shriek of dismay, however, as the little man made at him with the rush and roar of a cannon ball. In Bailey's amazed eyes he seemed to bounce galvanically, landing on Joy's back with such vicious suddenness that the breath fled from him in a squawk of terror; then, seizing his cue, he kicked and belaboured the prostrate Celestial in feverish silence. He desisted and rolled across the porch to Bailey. Staring truculently up et the landlord, he spoke for the first time.

"Was I right in supposin' that something amused you?"

Bailey gasped incredulously, for the voice rumbled heavily an octave below his own bass. Either the look of the stocky catapult, as he launched himself on the fleeing servant, or the invidious servility of the innkeeper, sobered the landlord, and he answered gravely:

"No, sir; I reckon you're mistaken. I ain't observed anything frivolous yet."

"Glad of it," said the little man. "I don't like a feller to hog a joke all by himself. Some of the Bar X boys took to absorbin' humour out of my shape when I first went to work, but they're sort of educated out of it now. I got an eye from one and a finger off of another; the last one donated a ear."

Bailey readily conceived this man as a bad antagonist, for the heavy corded neck had split buttons from the blue shirt, and he glimpsed a chest hairy, and round as a drum, while the brown arms showed knotty and hardened.

"Let's liquor," he said, and led the way into the big, low room, serving as bar, dining- and living-room. From the rear came vicious clatterings and slammings of pots, mingled with Oriental lamentations, indicating an aching body rather than a chastened spirit.

"Don't see you often," he continued, with a touch of implied curiosity, which grew as his guest, with lingering fondness, up-ended a glass brimful of the raw, fiery spirits.

"No, the old man don't lemme get away much. He knows that dwellin' close to the ground, as I do, I pine for spiritual elevation," with a melting glance at the bottles behind the bar, doing much to explain the size of his first drink.

"Like it, do ye?" questioned Bailey indicating the shelf.

"Well, not exactly! Booze is like air - I need it. It makes a new man out of me - and usually ends by gettin' both me and the new one laid off."

"Didn't hear nothing of the weddin' over at Los Huecos, did ye?"

"No! Whose weddin'?"

"Ross Turney, the new sheriff."

"Ye don't say! Him that's been elected on purpose to round up the Tremper gang, hey? Who's his antagonist?"

"Old man Miller's gal. He's celebratin' his election by gettin' spliced. I been expectin' of 'em across this way to-night, but I guess they took the Black Butte trail. You heard what he said, didn't ye? Claims that inside of ninety days he'll rid the county of the Trempers and give the reward to his wife for a bridal present. Five thousand dollars on 'em, you know." Bailey grinned evilly and continued: "Say! Marsh Tremper'll ride up to his house some night and make him eat his own gun in front of his bride, see if he don't. Then there'll be cause for an inquest and an election." He spoke with what struck the teamster as unnecessary heat.

"Dunno," said the other; "Turney's a brash young feller, I hear, but he's game. 'Tain't any of my business, though, and I don't want none of his contrac'. I'm violently addicted to peace and quiet, I am. Guess I'll unhitch," and he toddled out into the gathering dusk to his mules, while the landlord peered uneasily down the darkening trail.

As the saddened Joy lit candles in the front room there came the rattle of wheels without, and a buckboard stopped in the bar of light from the door. Bailey's anxiety was replaced by a mask of listless surprise as the voice of Ross Turney called to him.

"Hello there, Bailey! Are we in time for supper? If not, I'll start an insurrection with that Boxer of yours. He's got to turn out the snortingest supper of the season to-night. It isn't every day your shack is honoured by a bride. Mr. Bailey, this is my wife, since ten o'clock A. M." He introduced a blushing, happy girl, evidently in the grasp of many emotions. "We'll stay all night, I guess,"

"Sure," said Bailey. "I'll show ye a room," and he led them up beneath the low roof where an unusual cleanliness betrayed the industry of Joy.

The two men returned and drank to the bride, Turney with the reckless lightness that distinguished him, Bailey sullen and watchful.

"Got another outfit here, haven't you?" questioned the bridegroom. "Who is it?"

Before answer could be made, from the kitchen arose a tortured howl and the smashing of dishes, mingled with stormy rumblings. The door burst inward, and an agonized Joy fled, flapping out into the night, while behind him rolled the caricature from Bar X.

"I just stopped for a drink of water," boomed the dwarf, then paused at the twitching face of the sheriff.

He swelled ominously, like a great pigeon, purple and congested with rage. Strutting to the new-comer, he glared insolently up into his smiling face,

"What are ye laughin' at, ye shavetail?" His hands were clenched, till his arms showed tense and rigid, and the cords in his neck were thickly swollen.

"Lemme in on it, I'm strong on humour. What in - ails ye?" he yelled, in a fury, as the tall young man gazed fixedly, and the glasses rattled at the bellow from the barreled-up lungs.

"I'm not laughing at you," said the sheriff.

"Oh, ain't ye?" mocked the man of peace. "Well, take care that ye don't, ye big wart, or I'll trample them new clothes and browse around on some of your features. I'll take ye apart till ye look like cut feed. Guess ye don't know who I am, do ye? I'm -"

"Who is this man, Ross?" came the anxious voice of the bride, descending the stairs.

The little man spun like a dancer, and, spying the girl, blushed to the colour of a prickly pear, then stammered painfully, while the sweat stood out under the labour of his discomfort:

"Just 'Shorty,' Miss," he finally quavered. "Plain 'Shorty' of the Bar X - er - a miserable, crawlin' worm for disturbin' of you." He rolled his eyes helplessly at Bailey, while he sopped with his crumpled sombrero at the glistening perspiration.

"Why didn't ye tell me?" he whispered ferociously at

the host, and the volume of his query carried to Joy, hiding out in the night.

"Mr. Shorty," said the sheriff gravely; "let me introduce my wife, Mrs. Turney."

The bride smiled sweetly at the tremulous little man, who broke and fled to a high bench in the darkest corner, where he dangled his short legs in a silent ecstasy of bashfulness.

"I reckon I'll have to rope that Chink, then blindfold and back him into the kitchen, if we git any supper," said Bailey, disappearing.

Later the Chinaman stole in to set the table, but he worked with hectic and fitful energy, a fearful eye always upon the dim bulk in the corner, and at a fancied move he shook with an ague of apprehension. Backing and sidling, he finally announced the meal, prepared to stampede madly at notice.

During the supper Shorty ate ravenously of whatever lay to his hand, but asked no favours. The agony of his shyness paralysed his huge vocal muscles till speech became a labour quite impossible.

To a pleasant remark of the bride he responded, but no sound issued, then breathing heavily into his larynx, the reply roared upon them like a burst of thunder, seriously threatening the gravity of the meal. He retired abruptly into moist and self-conscious silence, fearful of feasting his eyes on this disturbing loveliness.

As soon as compatible with decency, he slipped back to his bunk in the shed behind, and lay staring into the

Rex E. Beach

darkness, picturing the amazing occurrences of the evening. At the memory of her level glances he fell a-tremble and sighed ecstatically, prickling with a new, strange emotion. He lay till far into the night, wakeful and absorbed. He was able, to grasp the fact but dimly that all this dazzling perfection was for one man. Were it not manifestly impossible he supposed other men in other lands knew other ladies as beautiful, and it furthermore grew upon him blackly, in the thick gloom, that in all this world of womanly sweetness and beauty, no modicum of it was for the misshapen dwarf of the Bar X outfit. All his life he had fought furiously to uphold the empty shell of his dignity in the eyes of his comrades, yet always morbidly conscious of the difference in his body. Whisky had been his solace, his sweetheart. It changed him, raised and beatified him into the likeness of other men, and now, as he pondered, he was aware of a consuming thirst engendered by the heat of his earlier emotions. Undoubtedly it must be quenched.

He rose and stole quietly out into the big front room. Perhaps the years of free life in the open had bred a suspicion of walls, perhaps he felt his conduct would not brook discovery, perhaps habit, prompted him to take the two heavy Colts from their holsters and thrust them inside his trousers band.

He slipped across the room, silent and cavern-like, its blackness broken by the window squares of starry sky, till he felt the paucity of glassware behind the bar.

"Here's to Her," It burned delightfully.

"Here's to the groom." It tingled more alluringly.

"I'll drink what I can, and get back to the bunk before it works," he thought, and the darkness veiled the measure of his potations.

He started at a noise on the stairway. His senses not yet dulled, detected a stealthy tread. Not the careless step of a man unafraid, but the cautious rustle and halt of a marauder. Every nerve bristled to keenest alertness as the faint occasional sounds approached, passed the open end of the bar where he crouched, leading on to the window. Then a match flared, and the darkness rushed out as a candle wick sputtered.

Shorty stretched on tiptoe, brought his eye to the level of the bar, and gazed upon the horrent head of Bailey. He sighed thankfully, but watched with interest his strange behaviour.

Bailey moved the light across the window from left to right three times, paused, then wigwagged some code out into the night.

"He's signalling," mused Shorty. "Hope he gets through quick. I'm getting full." The fumes of the liquor were beating at his senses, and he knew that soon he would move with difficulty.

The man, however, showed no intention of leaving, for, his signals completed, he blew out the light, first listening for any sound from above, then his figure loomed black and immobile against the dim starlight of the window.

"Oh, Lord! I got to set down," and the watcher squatted upon the floor, bracing against the wall. His dulling perceptions were sufficiently acute to detect shuffling footsteps on the porch and the cautious unbarring of the door.

"Gettin' late for visitors," he thought, as he entered a blissful doze. "When they're abed, I'll turn in."

It seemed much later that a shot startled him. To his dizzy hearing came the sound of curses overhead, the stamp and shift of feet, the crashing fall of struggling men, and, what brought him unsteadily to his legs, the agonized scream of a woman. It echoed through the house, chilling him, and dwindled to an aching moan.

Something was wrong, he knew that, but it was hard to tell just what. He must think. What hard work it was to think, too; he'd never noticed before what a laborious process it was. Probably that sheriff had got into trouble; he was a fresh guy, anyhow; and he'd laughed when he first saw Shorty. That settled it. He could get out of it himself. Evidently it was nothing serious, for there was no more disturbance above, only confused murmurings. Then a light showed in the stairs, and again the shuffling of feet came, as four strange men descended. They were lighted by the sardonic Bailey, and they dragged a sixth between them, bound and helpless. It was the sheriff.

Now, what had he been doing to get into such a fix?

The prisoner stood against the wall, white and defiant. He strained at his bonds silently, while his captors watched his futile struggles. There was something terrible and menacing in the quietness with which they gloated - a suggestion of some horror to come. At last he desisted, and burst forth.

"You've got me all right. You did this, Bailey, you - traitor."

"He's never been a traitor, as far as we know," sneered one of the four. "In fact, I might say he's been strictly on the square with us."

"I didn't think you made war on women, either, Marsh Tremper, but it seems you're everything from a dog-thief down. Why couldn't you fight me alone, in the daylight, like a man?"

"You don't wait till a rattler's coiled before you stamp his head off," said the former speaker. "It's either you or us, and I reckon it's you."

So these were the Tremper boys, eh? The worst desperadoes in the Southwest; and Bailey was their ally. The watcher eyed them, mildly curious, and it seemed to him that they were as bad a quartette as rumour had painted - bad, even, for this country of bad men. The sheriff was a fool for getting mixed up with such people. Shorty knew enough to mind his own business, anyway, if others didn't. He was a peaceful man, and didn't intend to get mixed up with outlaws. His mellow meditations were interrupted by the hoarse speech of the sheriff, who had broken down into his rage again, and struggled madly while words ran from him.

"Let me go! - you, let me free. I want to fight the coward that struck my wife. You've killed her. Who was it? Let me get at him."

Shorty stiffened as though a douche of ice-water had struck him. "Killed her! Struck his wife!" My God!

Not that sweet creature of his dreams who had talked and smiled at him without noting his deformity -

An awful anger rose in him and he moved out into the light.

"Han'sup!"

Whatever of weakness may have dragged at his legs, none sounded in the great bellowing command that flooded the room. At the compelling volume of the sound every man whirled and eight empty hands shot skyward. Their startled eyes beheld a man's squat body weaving uncertainly on the limbs of an insect, while in each hand shone a blue-black Colt that waved and circled in maddening, erratic orbits.

At the command, Marsh Tremper's mind had leaped to the fact that behind him was one man; one against five, and he took a gambler's chance.

As he whirled, he drew and fired. None but the dwarf of Bar X could have lived, for he was the deadliest hip shot in the territory. His bullet crashed into the wall, a hand's breadth over Shorty's "cow-lick." It was a clean heart shot; the practised whirl and flip of the finished gun fighter; but the roar of his explosion was echoed by another, and the elder Tremper spun unsteadily against the table with a broken shoulder.

"Too high," moaned the big voice. " - The liquor."

He swayed drunkenly, but at the slightest shift of his quarry, the aimless wanderings of a black muzzle stopped on the spot and the body behind the guns was congested with deadly menace.

"Face the wall," he cried. "Quick! Keep 'em up higher!" They sullenly obeyed; their wounded leader reaching with his uninjured member.

To the complacent Shorty, it seemed that things were working nicely, though he was disturbingly conscious of his alcoholic lack of balance, and tortured by the fear that he might suddenly lose the iron grip of his faculties.

Then, for the second time that night, from the stairs came the voice that threw him into the dreadful confusion of his modesty.

"O Ross!" it cried, "I've brought your gun," and there on the steps, dishevelled, pallid and quivering, was the bride, and grasped in one trembling hand was her husband's weapon.

"Ah - h!" sighed Shorty, seraphically, as the vision beat in upon his misty conceptions. "*She ain't hurt!*"

In his mind there was no room for desperadoes contemporaneously with Her. Then he became conscious of the lady's raiment, and his brown cheeks flamed brick-red, while he dropped his eyes. In his shrinking, grovelling modesty, he made for his dark corner.

One of those at bay, familiar with this strange abashment, seized the moment, but at his motion the sheriff screamed: "Look out!"

The quick danger in the cry brought back with a surge the men against the wall and Shorty swung instantly, firing at the outstretched hand of Bailey as it reached for Tremper's weapon.

The landlord straightened, gazing affrightedly at his finger tips.

"Too low!" and Shorty's voice held aching tears. "I'll never touch another drop; it's plumb ruined my aim."

"Cut these strings, girlie," said the sheriff, as the little man's gaze again wavered, threatening to leave his prisoners.

"Quick. He's blushing again.".

When they were manacled, Shorty stood in moist exudation, trembling and speechless, under the incoherent thanks of the bride and the silent admiration of her handsome husband. She fluttered about him in a tremor of anxiety, lest he be wounded, caressing him here and there with solicitous pats till he felt his shamed and happy spirit would surely burst from its misshapen prison.

"You've made a good thing to-night," said Turney, clapping him heartily on his massive back. "You get the five thousand all right. We were going to Mexico City on that for a bridal trip when I rounded up the gang, but I'll see you get every cent of it, old man. If it wasn't for you I'd have been a heap farther south than that by now."

The open camaraderie and good-fellowship that rang in the man's voice affected Shorty strangely, accustomed as he was to the veiled contempt or open compassion of his fellows. Here was one who recognized him as a man, an equal.

He spread his lips, but the big voice squeaked

dismally, then, inflating deeply, he spoke so that the prisoners chained in the corral outside heard him plainly.

"I'd rather she took it anyhow," blushing violently.

"No, no," they cried. "It's yours."

"Well, then, half of it" - and for once Shorty betrayed the strength of Gibraltar, even in the face of the lady, and so it stood.

As the dawn spread over the dusty prairie, tipping the westward mountains with silver caps, and sucking the mist out of the cotton-wood bottoms, he bade them adieu.

"No, I got to get back to the Bar X, or the old man'll swear I been drinking again, and I don't want to dissipate no wrong impressions around." He winked gravely. Then, as the sheriff and his surly prisoners drove off, he called:

"Mr. Turney, take good care of them Trempers. I think a heap of 'em, for, outside of your wife, they're the only ones in this outfit that didn't laugh at me."

THE TEST

Pierre "Feroce" showed disapproval in his every attitude as plainly as disgust peered from the seams in his dark face; it lurked in his scowl and in the curl of his long rawhide that bit among the sled dogs. So at least thought Willard, as he clung to the swinging sledge.

They were skirting the coast, keeping to the glare ice, wind-swept and clean, that lay outside the jumbled shore pack. The team ran silently in the free gait of the grey wolf, romping in harness from pure joy of motion and the intoxication of perfect life, making the sled runners whine like the song of a cutlass.

This route is dangerous, of course, from hidden cracks in the floes, and most travellers hug the bluffs, but he who rides with Pierre "Feroce" takes chances. It was this that had won him the name of "Wild" Pierre - the most reckless, tireless man of the trails, a scoffer at peril, bolting through danger with rush and frenzy, overcoming sheerly by vigour those obstacles which destroy strong men in the North.

The power that pulsed within him gleamed from his eyes, rang in his song, showed in the aggressive thrust of his sensual face.

This particular morning, however, Pierre's distemper had crystallized into a great contempt for his companion. Of all trials, the most detestable is to hit the trail with half a man, a pale, anemic weakling like this stranger.

Though modest in the extent of his learning, Pierre gloated in a freedom of speech, the which no man dared deny him. He turned to eye his companion cynically for a second time, and contempt was patent in his gaze. Willard appeared slender and pallid in his furs, though his clear-cut features spoke a certain strength and much refinement.

"Bah! I t'ink you dam poor feller," he said finally. "'Ow you 'goin' stan' thees trip, eh? She's need beeg mans, not leetle runt like you."

Amusement at this frankness glimmered in Willard's eyes.

"You're like all ignorant people. You think in order to stand hardship a man should be able to toss a sack of flour in his teeth or juggle a cask of salt-horse."

"Sure t'ing," grinned Pierre. "That's right. Look at me. Mebbe you hear 'bout Pierre 'Feroce' sometime, eh?"

"Oh, yes; everybody knows you; knows you're a big bully. I've seen you drink a quart of this wood alcohol they call whisky up here, and then jump the bar from a stand, but you're all animal - you haven't the refinement and the culture that makes real strength. It's the mind that makes us stand punishment."

"Ha! ha! ha!" laughed the Canadian. "Wat a fonny talk.

She'll take the heducate man for stan' the col', eh? Mon Dieu!" He roared again till the sled dogs turned fearful glances backward and bushy tails drooped under the weight of their fright. Great noise came oftenest with great rage from Pierre, and they had too frequently felt the both to forget.

"Yes, you haven't the mentality. Sometime you'll use up your physical resources and go to pieces like a burned wick."

Pierre was greatly amused. His yellow teeth shone, and he gave vent to violent mirth as, following the thought, he pictured a naked mind wandering over the hills with the quicksilver at sixty degrees.

"Did you ever see a six-day race? Of course not; you barbarians haven't sunk to the level of our dissolute East, where we joy in Roman spectacles, but if you had you'd see it's will that wins; it's the man that eats his soul by inches. The educated soldier stands the campaign best. You run too much to muscle - you're not balanced."

"I t'ink mebbe you'll 'ave chance for show 'im, thees stout will of yours. She's goin' be long 'mush' troo the mountains, plentee snow, plentee cold."

Although Pierre's ridicule was galling, Willard felt the charm of the morning too strongly to admit of anger or to argue his pet theory.

The sun, brilliant and cold, lent a paradoxical cheerfulness to the desolation, and, though never a sign of life broke the stillness around them, the beauty of the scintillant, gleaming mountains, distinct as cameos, that guarded the bay, appealed to him with the strange attraction of the Arctics; that attraction that calls and calls insistently, till men forsake God's country for its mystery.

He breathed the biting air cleaned by leagues of lifeless barrens and voids of crackling frost till he ached with the exhilaration of a perfect morning on the Circle.

Also before him undulated the grandest string of dogs the Coast had known. Seven there were, tall and grey, with tails like plumes, whom none but Pierre could lay hand upon, fierce and fearless as their master. He drove with the killing cruelty of a stampeder, and they loved him.

"You say you have grub cached at the old Indian hut on the Good Hope?" questioned Willard.

"Sure! Five poun' bacon, leetle flour and rice. I cache one gum-boot too, ha! Good thing for make fire queeck, eh?"

"You bet; an old rubber boot comes handy when it's too cold to make shavings."

Leaving the coast, they ascended a deep and tortuous river where the snow lay thick and soft. One man on snow-shoes broke trail for the dogs till they reached the foothills. It was hard work, but infinitely preferable to that which followed, for now they came into a dangerous stretch of overflows. The stream, frozen to its bed, clogged the passage of the spring water beneath, forcing it up through cracks till it spread over the solid ice, forming pools and sheets covered with treacherous ice-skins. Wet feet are fatal to man and beast, and they made laborious detours, wallowing trails through tangled willows waist deep in the snow smother, or clinging precariously to the overhanging bluffs. As they reached the river's source the sky blackened suddenly, and great clouds of snow rushed over the bleak hills, boiling down into the valley with a furious draught. They flung up their flimsy tent, only to have it flattened by the force of the gale that cut like well-honed steel. Frozen spots leaped out white on their faces, while their hands stiffened ere they could fasten the guy strings.

Finally, having lashed the tent bottom to the protruding willow tops, by grace of heavy lifting they strained their flapping shelter up sufficiently to crawl within.

"By Gar! She's blow hup ver' queeck," yelled Pierre, as he set the ten-pound sheet-iron stove, its pipe swaying drunkenly with the heaving tent.

"Good t'ing she hit us in the brush." He spoke as calmly as though danger was distant, and a moment later the little box was roaring with its oil-soaked kindlings.

"Will this stove burn green willow tops?" cried Willard.

"Sure! She's good stove. She'll burn hicicles eef you get 'im start one times. See 'im get red?"

They rubbed the stiff spots from their cheeks, then, seizing the axe, Willard crawled forth into the storm and dug at the base of the gnarled bushes. Occasionally a shrub assumed the proportions of a man's wrist - but rarely. Gathering an armful, he bore them inside, and twisting the tips into withes, he fed the fire. The frozen twigs sizzled and snapped, threatening to fail utterly, but with much blowing he sustained a blaze sufficient to melt a pot of snow. Boiling was out of the question, but the tea leaves became soaked and the bacon cauterized.

Pierre freed and fed the dogs. Each gulped its dried salmon, and, curling in the lee of the tent, was quickly drifted over. Next he cut blocks from the solid bottom snow and built a barricade to windward. Then he accumulated a mow of willow tops without the tent-fly. All the time the wind drew down the valley like the breath of a giant bellows.

"Supper," shouted Willard, and as Pierre crawled into the candle-light he found him squatted, fur-bundled, over the stove, which settled steadily into the snow, melting its way downward toward a firmer foundation.

The heat was insufficient to thaw the frozen sweat in his clothes; his eyes were bleary and wet from smoke, and his nose needed continuous blowing, but he spoke pleasantly, a fact which Pierre noted with approval.

"We'll need a habeas corpus for this stove if you don't get something to hold her up, and I might state, if it's worthy of mention, that your nose is frozen again."

Pierre brought an armful of stones from the creek edge, distributing them beneath the stove on a bed of twisted willows; then swallowing their scanty, half-cooked food, they crawled, shivering, into the deerskin sleeping-bags, that animal heat might dry their clammy garments.

Four days the wind roared and the ice filings poured over their shelter while they huddled beneath. When one travels on rations delay is dangerous. Each morning, dragging themselves out into the maelstrom, they took sticks and poked into the drifts for dogs. Each animal as found was exhumed, given a fish, and became straightway reburied in the whirling white that seethed down from the mountains.

On the fifth, without warning, the storm died, and the air stilled to a perfect silence.

"These dog bad froze," said Pierre, swearing earnestly as he harnessed. "I don' like eet much. They goin' play hout I'm 'fraid." He knelt and chewed from between their toes the ice pellets that had accumulated. A malamoot is hard pressed to let his feet mass, and this added to the men's uneasiness.

As they mounted the great divide, mountains rolled away on every hand, barren, desolate, marble-white; always the whiteness; always the listening silence that oppressed like a weight. Myriads of creek valleys radiated below in a bewildering maze of twisting seams.

"Those are the Ass's Ears, I suppose," said Willard, gazing at two great fangs that bit deep into the sky-line. "Is it true that no man has ever reached them?"

"Yes. The hinjun say that's w'ere hall the storm come from, biccause w'en the win' blow troo the Ass's Ear, look out! Somebody goin' ketch 'ell."

Dogs' feet wear quickly after freezing, for crusted snow cuts like a knife. Spots of blood showed in their tracks, growing more plentiful till every print was a crimson stain. They limped pitifully on their raw pads, and occasionally one whined. At every stop they sank in track, licking their lacerated paws, rising only at the cost of much whipping.

On the second night, faint and starved, they reached the hut. Digging away the drifts, they crawled inside to find it half full of snow - snow which had sifted through the crevices. Pierre groped among the shadows and swore excitedly.

"What's up?" said Willard.

Vocal effort of the simplest is exhausting when spent with hunger, and these were the first words he had spoken for hours.

"By Gar! she's gone. Somebody stole my grub!"

Willard felt a terrible sinking, and his stomach cried for food.

"How far is it to the Crooked River Road House?"

"One long day drive - forty mile."

"We must make it to-morrow or go hungry, eh? Well this isn't the first dog fish I ever ate." Both men gnawed a mouldy dried salmon from their precious store.

As Willard removed his footgear he groaned.

"Wat's the mattaire?"

"I froze my foot two days ago - snow-shoe strap too tight." He exhibited a heel, from which, in removing his inner sock, the flesh and skin had come away.

"That's all right," grinned Pierre. "You got the beeg will lef' yet. It take the heducate man for stan' the col', you know."

Willard gritted his teeth.

They awoke to the whine of a grey windstorm that swept the cutting snow in swirling clouds and made travel a madness. The next day was worse.

Two days of hunger weigh heavy when the cold weakens, and they grew gaunt and fell away in their features.

"I'm glad we've got another feed for the dogs," remarked Willard. "We can't let them run hungry, even if we do."

"I t'ink she's be hall right to-mor'," ventured Pierre. "Thees ain't snow - jus' win'; bimeby all blow hout. Sacre! I'll can eat 'nuff for 'ole harmy."

For days both men had been cold, and the sensation of complete warmth had come to seem strange and unreal, while their faces cracked where the spots had been.

Willard felt himself on the verge of collapse. He recalled his words about strong men, gazing the while at Pierre. The Canadian evinced suffering only in the haggard droop of eye and mouth; otherwise he looked strong and dogged.

Willard felt his own features had shrunk to a mask of loose-jawed suffering, and he set his mental sinews, muttering to himself.

He was dizzy and faint as he stretched himself in the still morning air upon waking, and hobbled painfully, but as his companion emerged from the darkened shelter into the crystalline brightness he forgot his own misery at sight of him. The big man reeled as though struck when the dazzle from the hills reached him, and he moaned, shielding his sight. Snow-blindness had found him in a night.

Slowly they plodded out of the valley, for hunger gnawed acutely, and they left a trail of blood tracks from the dogs. It took the combined efforts of both men to lash them to foot after each pause. Thus progress was slow and fraught with agony.

As they rose near the pass, miles of Arctic wastes bared themselves. All about towered bald domes, while everywhere stretched the monotonous white, the endless snow unbroken by tree or shrub, pallid and menacing, maddening to the eye.

"Thank God, the worst's over," sighed Willard, flinging himself onto the sled. "We'll make it to the summit next time; then she's down hill all the way to the road house."

Pierre said nothing.

Away to the northward glimmered the Ass's Ears, and as the speaker eyed them carelessly he noted gauzy shreds and streamers veiling their tops. The phenomena interested him, for he knew that here must be wind - wind, the terror of the bleak tundra; the hopeless, merciless master of the barrens! However, the distant range beneath the twin peaks showed clear-cut and distinct against the sky, and he did not mention the occurrence to the guide, although he recalled the words of the Indians: "Beware of the wind through the Ass's Ears."

Again they laboured up the steep slope, wallowing in the sliding snow, straining silently at the load; again they threw themselves, exhausted, upon it. Now, as he eyed the panorama below, it seemed to have suffered a subtle change, indefinable and odd. Although but a few minutes had elapsed, the coast mountains no longer loomed clear against the horizon, and his visual range appeared foreshortened, as though the utter distances had lengthened, bringing closer the edge of things. The twin peaks seemed endlessly distant and hazy, while the air had thickened as though congested with possibilities, lending a remoteness to the landscape.

"If it blows up on us here, we're gone," he thought, "for it's miles to shelter, and we're right in the saddle of the hills."

Pierre, half blinded as he was, arose uneasily and cast the air like a wild beast, his great head thrown back, his nostrils quivering.

"I smell the win'," he cried. "Mon Dieu! She's goin' blow!"

A volatile pennant floated out from a near-bye peak, hanging about its crest like faint smoke. Then along the brow of the pass writhed a wisp of drifting, twisting flakelets, idling hither and yon, astatic and aimless, settling in a hollow. They sensed a thrill and rustle to the air, though never a breath had touched them; then, as they mounted higher, a draught fanned them, icy as interstellar space. The view from the summit was grotesquely distorted, and glancing upward they found the guardian peaks had gone a-smoke with clouds of snow that whirled confusedly, while an increasing breath sucked over the summit, stronger each second. Dry snow began to rustle slothfully about their feet. So swiftly were the changes wrought, that before the mind had grasped their import the storm was on them, roaring down from every side, swooping out of the boiling sky, a raging blast from the voids of sunless space.

Pierre's shouts as he slashed at the sled lashings were snatched from his lips in scattered scraps. He dragged forth the whipping tent and threw himself upon it with the sleeping-bags. Having cut loose the dogs, Willard crawled within his sack and they drew the flapping canvas over them. The air was twilight and heavy with efflorescent granules that hurtled past in a drone.

They removed their outer garments that the fur might fold closer against them, and lay exposed to the full hate of the gale. They hoped to be drifted over, but no snow could lodge in this hurricane, and it sifted past, dry and sharp, eddying out a bare place wherein they lay. Thus the wind drove the chill to their bones bitterly.

An unnourished human body responds but weakly, so, vitiated by their fast and labours, their suffering smote them with tenfold cruelty.

All night the north wind shouted, and, as the next day

waned with its violence undiminished, the frost crept in upon them till they rolled and tossed shivering. Twice they essayed to crawl out, but were driven back to cower for endless, hopeless hours.

It is in such black, aimless times that thought becomes distorted. Willard felt his mind wandering through bleak dreams and tortured fancies, always to find himself harping on his early argument with Pierre: "It's the mind that counts." Later he roused to the fact that his knees, where they pressed against the bag, were frozen; also his feet were numb and senseless. In his acquired consciousness he knew that along the course of his previous mental vagary lay madness, and the need of action bore upon him imperatively.

He shouted to his mate, but "Wild" Pierre seemed strangely apathetic.

"We've got to run for it at daylight. We're freezing. Here! Hold on! What are you doing? Wait for daylight!" Pierre had scrambled stiffly out of his cover and his gabblings reached Willard. He raised a clenched fist into the darkness of the streaming night, cursing horribly with words that appalled the other.

"Man! man! don't curse your God. This is bad enough as it is. Cover up. Quick!"

Although apparently unmindful of his presence, the other crawled back muttering.

As the dim morning greyed the smother they rose and fought their way downward toward the valley. Long since they had lost their griping hunger, and now held only an apathetic indifference to food, with a cringing dread of the cold and a stubborn sense of their extreme necessity.

They fell many times, but gradually drew themselves more under control, the exercise suscitating them, as they staggered downward, blinded and buffeted, their only hope the road-house.

Willard marvelled dully at the change in Pierre. His face had shrivelled to blackened freezes stretched upon a bony substructure, and lighted by feverish, glittering, black, black eyes. It seemed to him that his own lagging body had long since failed, and that his aching, naked soul wandered stiffly through the endless day. As night approached Pierre stopped frequently, propping himself with legs far apart; sometimes he laughed. Invariably this horrible sound shocked Willard into a keener sense of the surroundings, and it grew to irritate him, for the Frenchman's mental wanderings increased with the darkness. What made him rouse one with his awful laughter? These spells of walking insensibility were pleasanter far. At last the big man fell. To Willard's mechanical endeavours to help he spoke sleepily, but with the sanity of a man under great stress.

"Dat no good. I'm goin' freeze right 'ere - freeze stiff as 'ell. Au revoir."

"Get up!" Willard kicked him weakly, then sat upon the prostrate man as his own faculties went wandering.

Eventually he roused, and digging into the snow buried the other, first covering his face with the ample parka hood. Then he struck down the valley. In one lucid spell he found he had followed a sled trail, which was blown clear and distinct by the wind that had now almost died away.

Occasionally his mind grew clear, and his pains beat in upon him till he grew furious at the life in him which refused to end, which forced him ever through this gauntlet of misery. More often he was conscious only of a vague and terrible extremity outside of himself that goaded him forever forward. Anon he strained to recollect his destination. His features had set in an implacable grimace of physical torture – like a runner in the fury of a finish - till the frost hardened them so. At times he fell heavily, face downward, and at length upon the trail, lying so till that omnipresent coercion that had frozen in his brain drove him forward.

He heard his own voice maundering through lifeless lips like that of a stranger: "The man that can eat his soul will win, Pierre."

Sometimes he cried like a child and slaver ran from his open mouth, freezing at his breast. One of his hands was going dead. He stripped the left mitten off and drew it laboriously over the right. One he would save at least, even though he lost the other. He looked at the bare member dully, and he could not tell that the cold had eased till the bitterness was nearly out of the air. He laboured with the fitful spurts of a machine run down.

Ten men and many dogs lay together in the Crooked River Road House through the storm. At late bedtime of the last night came a scratching on the door.

"Somebody's left a dog outside," said a teamster, and rose to let him in. He opened the door only to retreat affrightedly.

"My God!" he said. "My God!" and the miners crowded forward.

A figure tottered over the portal, swaying drunkenly. They shuddered at the sight of its face as it crossed toward the fire. It did not walk; it shuffled, haltingly, with flexed knees and hanging shoulders, the strides measuring inches only - a grisly burlesque upon senility.

Pausing in the circle, it mumbled thickly, with great effort, as though gleaning words from infinite distance:

"Wild Pierre - frozen - buried - in - snow - hurry!" Then he straightened and spoke strongly, his voice flooding the room:

"It's the mind, Pierre. Ha! ha! ha! The mind."

He cackled hideously, and plunged forward into a miner's arms.

It was many days before his delirium broke. Gradually he felt the pressure of many bandages upon him, and the hunger of convalescence. As he lay in his bunk the past came to him hazy and horrible; then the hum of voices, one loud, insistent, and familiar.

He turned weakly, to behold Pierre propped in a chair by the stove, frost-scarred and pale, but aggressive even in recuperation. He gesticulated fiercely with a bandaged hand, hot in controversy with some big-limbed, bearded strangers.

"Bah! You fellers no good - too beeg in the ches', too leetle in the forehead. She'll tak' the heducate mans for stan' the 'ardsheep - lak' me an' Meestaire Weelard."

NORTH OF FIFTY-THREE

Big George was drinking, and the activities of the little Arctic mining camp were paralysed. Events invariably ceased their progress and marked time when George became excessive, and now nothing of public consequence stirred except the quicksilver, which was retiring fearfully into its bulb at the song of the wind which came racing over the lonesome, bitter, northward waste of tundra.

He held the centre of the floor at the Northern Club, and proclaimed his modest virtues in a voice as pleasant as the cough of a bull-walrus.

"Yes, me! Little Georgie! I did it. I've licked 'em all from Herschel Island to Dutch Harbour, big uns and little uns. When they didn't suit I made 'em over. I'm the boss carpenter of the Arctic and I own this camp; don't I, Slim? Hey? Answer me!" he roared at the emaciated bearer of the title, whose attention seemed wandering from the inventory of George's startling traits toward a card game.

"Sure ye do," nervously smiled Slim, frightened out of a heart-solo as he returned to his surroundings.

"Well, then, listen to what I'm saying. I'm the big chief of the village, and when I'm stimulated and happy

Rex E. Beach

them fellers I don't like hides out and lets me and Nature operate things. Ain't that right?" He glared inquiringly at his friends.

Red, the proprietor, explained over the bar in a whisper to Captain, the new man from Dawson: "That's Big George, the whaler. He's a squaw-man and sort of a bully - see? When he's sober he's on the level strickly, an' we all likes him fine, but when he gets to fightin' the pain-killer, he ain't altogether a gentleman. Will he fight? Oh! Will he fight? Say! he's there with chimes, he is! Why, Doc Miller's made a grub-stake rebuildin' fellers that's had a lingerin' doubt cached away about that, an' now when he gets the booze up his nose them patched-up guys oozes away an' hibernates till the gas dies out in him. Afterwards he's sore on himself an' apologizes to everybody. Don't get into no trouble with him, cause he's two checks past the limit. They don't make 'em as bad as him any more. He busted the mould."

George turned, and spying the new-comer, approached, eyeing him with critical disfavour.

Captain saw a bear-like figure, clad cap-a-pie in native fashion. Reindeer pants, with the hair inside, clothed legs like rock pillars, while out of the loose squirrel parka a corded neck rose, brown and strong, above which darkly gleamed a rugged face seamed and scarred by the hate of Arctic winters. He had kicked off his deer-skin socks, and stood bare-footed on the cold and draughty floor, while the poison he had imbibed showed only in his heated face, Silently he extended a cracked and hardened hand, which closed like the armoured claw of a crustacean and tightened on the crunching fingers of the other. Captain's expression remained unchanged and, gradually slackening his grip, the sailor roughly inquired:

"Where'd you come from?"

"Just got in from Dawson yesterday," politely responded the stranger.

"Well! what're you goin' to do now you're here?" he demanded.

"Stake some claims and go to prospecting, I guess. You see, I wanted to get in early before the rush next spring."

"Oh! I 'spose you're going to jump some of our ground, hey? Well, you ain't! We don't want no claim jumpers here," disagreeably continued the seaman; "we won't stand for it. This is my camp - see? I own it, and these is my little children." Then, as the other refused to debate with him, he resumed, groping for a new ground of attack.

"Say! I'll bet you're one of them eddicated dudes, too, ain't you? You talk like a feller that had been to college," and, as the other assented, he scornfully called to his friends, saying "Look here, fellers! Pipe the jellyfish! I never see one of these here animals that was worth a cuss; they plays football an' smokes cigareets at school; then when they're weaned they come off up here an' jump our claims 'cause we can't write a location notice proper. They ain't no good. I guess I'll stop it."

Captain moved toward the door, but the whaler threw his bulky frame against it and scowlingly blocked the way.

"No, you don't. You ain't goin' to run away till I've had the next dance, Mister Eddication! Humph! I ain't begun to tell ye yet what a useless little barnacle you are."

Red interfered, saying: "Look 'ere, George, this guy ain't no playmate of yourn. We'll all have a jolt of this disturbance promoter, an' call it off." Then, as the others approached he winked at Captain, and jerked his head slightly toward the door.

The latter, heeding the signal, started out, but George leaped after him and, seizing an arm, whirled him back, roaring:

"Well, of all the cussed impidence I ever see! You're too high-toned to drink with us, are you? You don't get out of here now till you take a lickin' like a man."

He reached over his head and, grasping the hood of his fur shirt, with one movement he stripped it from him, exposing a massive naked body, whose muscles swelled and knotted beneath a skin as clear as a maiden's, while a map of angry scars strayed across the heavy chest.

As the shirt sailed through the air. Red lightly vaulted to the bar and, diving at George's naked middle, tackled beautifully, crying to Captain: "Get out quick; we'll hold him."

Others rushed forward and grasped the bulky sailor, but Captain's voice replied: "I sort of like this place, and I guess I'll stay a while. Turn him loose."

"Why, man, he'll kill ye," excitedly cried Slim. "Get out!"

The captive hurled his peacemakers from him and, shaking off the clinging arms, drove furiously at the insolent stranger.

In the cramped limits of the corner where he stood. Captain was unable to avoid the big man, who swept him with a crash against the plank door at his back, grasping hungrily at his throat. As his shoulders struck, however, he dropped to his knees and, before the raging George could seize him, he avoided a blow which would have strained the rivets of a strength-tester and ducked under the other's arms, leaping to the cleared centre of the floor.

Seldom had the big man's rush been avoided and, whirling, he swung a boom-like arm at the agile stranger. Before it landed, Captain stepped in to meet his adversary and, with the weight of his body behind the blow, drove a clenched and bony fist crashing into the other's face. The big head with its blazing shock of hair snapped backward and the whaler drooped to his knees at the other's feet.

The drunken flush of victory swept over Captain as he stood above the swaying figure; then, suddenly, he felt the great bare arms close about his waist with a painful grip. He struck at the bleeding face below him and wrenched at the circling bands which wheezed the breath from his lungs, but the whaler squeezed him writhing to his breast, and, rising, unsteadily wheeled across the floor and in a shiver of broken glass fell crashing against the bar and to the floor.

As the struggling men writhed upon the planks the door opened at the hurried entrance of an excited group, which paused at the sight of the ruin, then, rushing forward, tore the men apart.

The panting Berserker strained at the arms about his glistening body, while Captain, with sobbing sighs, relieved his aching lungs and watched his enemy, who frothed at the interference.

"It was George's fault," explained Slim to the questions of the arrivals. "This feller tried to make a get-away, but George had to have his amusement."

A new-comer addressed the squaw-man in a voice as cold as the wind. "Cut this out, George! This is a friend of mine. You're making this camp a regular hell for strangers, and now I'm goin' to tap your little snap. Cool off - see?"

Jones's reputation as a bad gun-man went hand in hand with his name as a good gambler, and his scanty remarks invariably evoked attentive answers, so George explained: "I don't like him Jones, and I was jus' makin' him over to look like a man. I'll do it yet, too," he flashed wrathfully at his quiet antagonist.

"'Pears to me like he's took a hand in the remodelling himself," replied the gambler, "but if you're lookin' for something to do, here's your chance. Windy Jim just drove in and says Barton and Kid Sullivan are adrift on the ice."

"What's that?" questioned eager voices, and, forgetting the recent trouble at the news, the crowd pressed forward anxiously.

"They was crossing the bay and got carried out by the off-shore gale," explained Jones. "Windy was follerin' 'em when the ice ahead parted and begun movin' out. He tried to yell to 'em, but they was too far away to hear in the storm. He managed to get back to the land and follered the shore ice around. He's over at Hunter's cabin now, most dead, face and hands froze pretty bad."

A torrent of questions followed and many suggestions as to the fate of the men.

"They'll freeze before they can get ashore," said one.

"The ice-pack'll break up in this wind," added another, "and if they don't drown, they'll freeze before the floe comes in close enough for them to land."

From the first announcement of his friends' peril, Captain had been thinking rapidly. His body, sore from his long trip and aching from the hug of his recent encounter, cried woefully for rest, but his voice rose calm and clear:

"We've got to get them off," he said. "Who will go with me? Three is enough."

The clamouring voices ceased, and the men wheeled at the sound, gazing incredulously at the speaker. "What!" - "In this storm?" - "You're crazy," many voices said.

He gazed appealingly at the faces before him. Brave and adventurous men he knew them to be, jesting with death, and tempered to perils in this land where hardship rises with the dawn, but they shook their ragged heads hopelessly.

"We *must* save them!" resumed Captain hotly. "Barton and I played as children together, and if there's not a man among you who's got the nerve to follow me - I'll go alone by Heavens!"

In the silence of the room, he pulled the cap about his ears and, tying it snugly under his chin, drew on his huge fur mittens; then with a scornful laugh he turned toward the door.

He paused as his eye caught the swollen face of Big George. Blood had stiffened in the heavy creases of his face like rusted stringers in a ledge, while his mashed and discoloured lips protruded thickly. His hair gleamed red, and the sweat had dried upon his naked shoulders, streaked with dirt and flecked with spots of blood, yet the battered features shone with the unconquered, fearless light of a rough, strong man.

Captain strode to him with outstretched hand. "You're a man," he said. "You've got the nerve, George, and you'll go with me, won't you?"

"What! Me?" questioned the sailor vaguely. His wondering glance left Captain, and drifted round the circle of shamed and silent faces - then he straightened stiffly and cried: "Will I go with you? Certainly! I'll go to - with you."

Ready hands harnessed the dogs, dragged from protected nooks where they sought cover from the storm which moaned and whistled round the low houses. Endless ragged folds of sleet whirled out of the north, then writhed and twisted past, vanishing into the grey veil which shrouded the landscape in a twilight gloom.

The fierce wind sank the cold into the aching flesh like a knife and stiffened the face to a whitening mask, while a fusillade of frozen ice-particles beat against the eyeballs with blinding fury.

As Captain emerged from his cabin, furred and hooded, he found a long train of crouching, whining animals harnessed and waiting, while muffled figures stocked the sled with robes and food and stimulants.

Big George approached through the whirling white, a great squat figure with fluttering squirrel tails blowing from his parka, and at his heels there trailed a figure, skin-clad and dainty.

"It's my wife," he explained briefly to Captain. "She won't let me go alone."

They gravely bade farewell to all, and the little crowd cheered lustily against the whine of the blizzard as, with cracking whip and hoarse shouts, they were wrapped in the cloudy winding sheet of snow.

Arctic storms have an even sameness; the intense cold, the heartless wind which augments tenfold the chill of the temperature, the air thick and dark with stinging flakes rushing by in an endless cloud. A drifting, freezing, shifting eternity of snow, driven by a ravening gale which sweeps the desolate, bald wastes of the Northland.

The little party toiled through the smother till they reached the "egloos" under the breast of the tall, coast bluffs, where coughing Eskimos drilled patiently at ivory tusks and gambled the furs from their backs at stud-horse poker.

To George's inquiries they answered that their largest canoe was the three-holed bidarka on the cache outside. Owing to the small circular openings in its deck, this was capable of holding but three passengers, and Captain said; "We'll have to make two trips, George."

"Two trips, eh?" answered the other. "We'll be doin' well if we last through one, I'm thinking."

Lashing the unwieldy burden upon the sled, they fought their way along the coast again till George declared they were opposite the point where their friends went adrift. They slid their light craft through the ragged wall of ice hummocks guarding the shore pack, and dimly saw, in the grey beyond them, a stretch of angry waters mottled by drifting cakes and floes.

George spoke earnestly to his wife, instructing her to keep the team in constant motion up and down the coast a rifle-shot in either direction, and to listen for a signal of the return. Then he picked her up as he would a babe, and she kissed his storm-beaten face.

"She's been a good squaw to me," he said, as they pushed their dancing craft out into the breath of the gale, "and I've always done the square thing by her; I s'pose she'll go back to her people now, though."

The wind hurried them out from land, while it drove the sea-water in freezing spray over their backs and changed their fur garments into scaly armour, as they worked through the ice cakes, peering with strained eyes for a sign of their friends.

The sailor, with deft strokes, steered them, between the grinding bergs, raising his voice in lone signals like the weird cry of a siren.

Twisting back and forth through the floes, they held to their quest, now floating with the wind, now paddling desperately in a race with some drifting mass which dimly towered above them and splintered hungrily against its neighbour close in their wake.

Captain emptied his six-shooter till his numbed fingers grew rigid as the trigger, and always at his back swelled the deep shouts of the sailor, who, with practised eye and mighty strokes, forced their way through the closing lanes between the jaws of the ice pack.

At last, beaten and tossed, they rested disheartened and hopeless. Then, as they drifted, a sound struggled to them against the wind - a faint cry, illusive and fleeting as a dream voice - and, still doubting, they heard it again.

"Thank God! We'll save 'em yet," cried Captain, and they drove the canoe boiling toward the sound.

Barton and Sullivan had fought the cold and wind stoutly hour after hour, till they found their great floe was breaking up in the heaving waters.

Then the horror of it had struck the Kid, till he raved and cursed up and down their little island, as it

Rex E. Beach

dwindled gradually to a small acre.

He had finally yielded to the weight of the cold which crushed resistance out of him, and settled, despairing and listless, upon the ice. Barton dragged him to his feet and forced him round their rocking prison, begging him to brace up, to fight it out like a man, till the other insisted on resting, and dropped to his seat again.

The older man struck deliberately at the whitening face of his freezing companion, who recognized the well-meant insult and refused to be roused into activity. Then to their ears had come the faint cries of George, and, in answer to their screams, through the gloom they beheld a long, covered, skin canoe, and the anxious faces of their friends.

Captain rose from his cramped seat, and, ripping his crackling garments from the boat where they had frozen, he wriggled out of the hole in the deck and grasped the weeping Barton.

"Come, come, old boy! It's all right now," he said.

"Oh, Charlie, Charlie!" cried the other. "I might have known you'd try to save us. You're just in time, though, for the Kid's about all in." Sullivan apathetically nodded and sat down again.

"Hurry up there; this ain't no G. A. R. Encampment, and you ain't got no time to spare," said George, who had dragged the canoe out and, with a paddle, broke the sheets of ice which covered it. "It'll be too dark to see anything in half an hour."

The night, hastened by the storm, was closing rapidly, and they realized another need of haste, for, even as they spoke, a crack had crawled through the ice-floe where they stood, and, widening as it went, left but a heaving cake supporting them.

George spoke quietly to Captain, while Barton strove to animate the Kid. "You and Barton must take him ashore and hurry him down to the village. He's most gone now."

"But you?" questioned the other. "We'll have to come back for you, as soon as we put him ashore."

"Never mind me," roughly interrupted George. "It's too late to get back here. When you get ashore it'll be dark. Besides Sullivan's freezing, and you'll have to rush him through quick. I'll stay here."

"No! No! George!" cried the other, as the meaning of it bore in upon him. "I got you into this thing, and it's my place to stay here. You must go -"

But the big man had hurried to Sullivan, and, seizing him in his great hands, shook the drowsy one like a rat, cursing and beating a goodly share of warmth back into him. Then he dragged the listless burden to the canoe and forced him to a seat in the middle opening.

"Come, come," he cried to the others; "you can't spend all night here. If you want to save the Kid, you've got to hurry. You take the front seat there, Barton," and, as he did so, George turned to the protesting Captain: "Shut up, curse you, and get in!"

"I won't do it," rebelled the other. "I can't let you lay

down your life in this way, when I made you come."

George thrust a cold face within an inch of the other's and grimly said: "If they hadn't stopped me, I'd beat you into dog-meat this morning, and if you don't quit this snivelling I'll do it yet. Now get in there and paddle to beat - or you'll never make it back. Quick!"

"I'll come back for you then, George, if I live to the shore," Captain cried, while the other slid the burdened canoe into the icy waters.

As they drove the boat into the storm, Captain realized the difficulty of working their way against the gale. On him fell the added burden of holding their course into the wind and avoiding the churning ice cakes. The spray whipped into his face like shot, and froze as it clung to his features. He strained at his paddle till the sweat soaked out of him and the cold air filled his aching lungs.

Unceasingly the merciless frost cut his face like a keen blade, till he felt the numb paralysis which told him his features were hardening under the touch of the cold.

An arm's length ahead the shoulders of the Kid protruded from the deck hole where he had sunk again into the death sleep, while Barton, in the forward seat, leaned wearily on his ice-clogged paddle, moaning as he strove to shelter his face from the sting of the blizzard.

An endless time they battled with the storm, slowly gaining, foot by foot, till in the darkness ahead they saw the wall of shore ice and swung into its partial shelter.

Dragging the now unconscious Sullivan from the boat, Captain rolled and threshed him, while Barton, too weak and exhausted to assist, feebly strove to warm his stiffened limbs.

In answer to their signals, the team appeared, maddened by the lash of the squaw. Then they wrapped Sullivan in warm robes, and forced scorching brandy down his throat, till he coughed weakly and begged them to let him rest.

"You must hurry him to the Indian village," directed Captain. "He'll only lose some fingers and toes now, maybe; but you've got to hurry!"

"Aren't you coming, too?" queried Barton. "We'll hire some Eskimos to go after George. I'll pay 'em anything."

"No, I'm going back to him now; he'd freeze before we could send help, and, besides, they wouldn't come out in the storm and the dark."

"But you can't work that big canoe alone. If you get out there and don't find him you'll never get back. Charlie! let me go, too," he said; then apologized. "I'm afraid I won't last, though; I'm too weak."

The squaw, who had questioned not at the absence of her lord, now touched Captain's arm. "Come," she said; "I go with you." Then addressing Barton, "You quick go Indian house; white man die, mebbe. Quick! I go Big George."

"Ah, Charlie, I'm afraid you'll never make it," cried Barton, and, wringing his friend's hand, he staggered into the darkness behind the sled wherein lay the fur-bundled Sullivan.

Captain felt a horror of the starving waters rise up in him and a panic shook him fiercely, till he saw the silent squaw waiting for him at the ice edge. He shivered as the wind searched through his dampened parka and hardened the wet clothing next to his body, but he took his place and dug the paddle fiercely into the water, till the waves licked the hair of his gauntlets.

The memory of that scudding trip through the darkness was always cloudy and visioned. Periods of keen alertness alternated with moments when his weariness bore upon him till he stiffly bent to his work, wondering what it all meant.

It was the woman's sharpened ear which caught the first answering cry, and her hands which steered the intricate course to the heaving berg where the sailor crouched, for, at their approach, Captain had yielded to the drowse of weariness and, in his relief at the finding, the blade floated from his listless hands.

He dreamed quaint dreams, broken by the chilling lash of spray from the strokes of the others, as they drove the craft back against the wind, and he only partly awoke from his lethargy when George wrenched him from his seat and forced him down the rough trail toward warmth and safety.

Soon, however, the stagnant blood tingled through his veins, and under the shelter of the bluffs they reached the village, where they found the anxious men waiting.

Skilful natives had worked the frost from Sullivan's

members, and the stimulants in the sled had put new life into Barton as well. So, as the three crawled wearily through the dog-filled tunnel of the egloo, they were met by two wet-eyed and thankful men, who silently wrung their hands or uttered broken words.

When they had been despoiled of their frozen furs, and the welcome heat of whisky and fire had met in their blood, Captain approached the whaler, who rested beside his mate.

"George, you're the bravest man I ever knew, and your woman is worthy of you," he said. He continued slowly, "I'm sorry about the fight this morning, too."

The big man rose and, crushing the extended palm in his grasp, said: "We'll just let that go double, partner. You're as game as I ever see." Then he added: "It was too bad them fellers interferred jest when they did - but we can finish it up whenever you say," and as the other, smiling, shook his head, he continued:

"Well, I'm glad of it, 'cause you'd sure beat me the next time."

WHERE NORTHERN LIGHTS
COME DOWN O' NIGHTS

The Mission House at Togiak stands forlornly on a wind-swept Alaskan spit, while huddled around it a swarm of dirt-covered "igloos" grovel in an ecstacy of abasement.

Many natives crawled out of these and stared across the bay as down a gully came an Arctic caravan, men and dogs, black against, the deadly whiteness. Ahead swung the guide, straddling awkwardly on his five foot webs, while the straining pack pattered at his heels. Big George, the driver, urged them with strong words, idioms of the Northland, and his long whip bit sharply at their legs.

His companion, clinging to the sled, stumbled now and then, while his face, splitting from the snap of the frost, was smothered in a muffler. Sometimes he fell, plunging into the snow, rising painfully, and groaning with the misery of "snow-blindness."

"Most there now. Cap, keep up your grit."

"I'm all right," answered the afflicted man, wearily. "Don't mind me."

George, too, had suffered from the sheen of the

unbroken whiteness, and, while his eyes had not wholly closed, he saw but dimly. His cheeks were grease-smeared, and blackened with charred wood to break the snow-glare, but through his mask showed signs of suffering, while his blood-shot eyes dripped scalding tears and throbbed distressfully. For days he had not dared to lose sight of the guide. Once he had caught him sneaking the dogs away, and he feared he had killed the man for a time. Now Jaska broke trail ahead, his sullen, swollen features baleful in their injury.

Down the steep bank they slid, across the humped up sea ice at the river mouth and into the village.

At the greeting of their guide to his tribesmen, George started. Twelve years of coast life had taught him the dialect from Point Barrow south, and he glanced at Captain to find whether he, too, had heard the message. As Jaska handed a talisman to the chief he strode to him and snatched it.

"Oho! It's Father Orloff, is it? D - him!" He gazed at the token, a white spruce chip with strange marks and carvings.

"What does it mean, George?" said the blind man.

"It's a long story, Charlie, and black. You should have known it before we started. I'm a marked man in this coast country. It's Orloff's work, the renegade. 'Father,' he calls himself. Father to these devils he rules and robs for himself in the name of the Church. His hate is bitter, and he'd have my life if these watery-livered curs didn't dread the sound of my voice. God help him when we meet."

He shook his hairy claws at the hostile circle, then cried to the chief in the native tongue: -

"Oh, Shaman! We come bleeding and weary. Hunger grips us and our bones are stiff with frost. The light is gone from my brother's eyes and we are sick. Open you the door to the Mission House that the 'Minoks' may rest and grow strong."

The Indians clustered before the portal, with its rude cross above, and stared malignantly, while the chief spoke. At the name of his enemy the unsightly eyes of George gleamed, and he growled contemptuously, advancing among them. They scattered at the manner of his coming, and he struck the padlocked door till it rattled stiffly. Then spying the cross overhead he lifted up and gripped the wood. It came away ripping, and with wails of rage and horror at the sacrilege, they closed about him.

"Here, Cap! Bust her in quick!" He dragged Captain before the entrance, thrusting the weapon upon him, then ran ferociously among the people. He snatched them to him, cuffing like a bear and trampling them into the snow. Those who came into the reach of his knotty arms crumpled up and twisted under his feet. He whirled into the group, roaring hoarsely, his angry, grease-blackened face hideous with rage. The aborigine is not a fighting machine; for him the side-step and counter have no being. They melted ahead of his blazing wrath, and he whisked them, fleeing, by their garments, so that they felt the stamp of his moccasined heels.

Captain dragged the team within, and George following, blocked the shattered door.

"We're safe as long as we stay in the Church," said he.

"Right of sanctuary, eh? Does it occur to you how we're going to get out?"

"Never mind, we'll get out somehow," said he, and that night, as Charlie Captain, late University man and engineer, lay with eyes swathed in steaming cloths, the whaler spoke operosely and with the bitterness of great wrong.

"It happened when we rocked the bars of Forty Mile, before ever a Chechako had crossed the Chilcoot. I went over to the headwaters of the Tanana. Into the big valley I went and got lost in the Flats. 'Tis a wild country, rimmed by high mountains, full of nigger-heads and tundra, with the river windin' clean back to the source of the Copper. I run out of grub. We always did them days, and built a raft to float down to the Yukon. A race with starvation, and a dead heat it near proved, too, though I had a shade the best of it. I drifted out into the main river, ravin' mad, my 'Mukluks' eat off and my moose-hide gun cover inside of me.

"A girl spied me from the village, and 'twas her brought me ashore in her birch-bark and tended me in her wick-i-up till reason came and the blood ran through me again.

"I mind seein' a white man stand around at times and hearin' him beg her to leave me to the old squaws. She didn't though. She gave me bits of moose meat and berries and dried salmon, and when I come to one day I saw she was little and brown and pleadin' and her clothes all covered with beads. Her eyes was big and sad, Cap, and dimples poked into her cheeks when she laughed.

"'Twas then that Orloff takes a hand - the white man. A priest he called himself; breed, Russian. Maybe he was, but a blacker hearted thief never wronged a child. He wanted the girl, Metla, and so did I. When I asked her old man for her he said she was promised to the Russian. I laughed at him, and a chief hates to be mocked. You know what sway the Church has over these Indians. Well, Orloff is a strong man. He held 'em like a rock. He worked on 'em till one day the tribemen came to me in a body and said, 'Go!'

"'Give me the girl, and I will,' says I.

"Orloff sneered. 'She was mine for a month before ye came,' says he with the fiend showin' back of his eyes. 'Do ye want her now?'

"For a minute I believed him. I struck once to kill, and he went down. They closed on me as fast as I shook 'em off. 'Twas a beautiful sight for a ruction, on the high banks over the river, but I was like water from the sickness. I fought to get at their priest where he lay, to stamp out his grinning face before they downed me, but I was beat back to the bluff and I battled with my heels over the edge. I broke a pole from the fish-rack and a good many went down. Then I heard Metla calling softly from below: -

"'Jump!' she said. 'Big one, jump.'

"She had loosed a canoe at the landing and now held it in the boiling current underneath, paddling desperately.

"As they ran out of the tents with their rifles I leaped.

"A long drop and cold water, but I hit feet first. When I rose the little girl was alongside.

"It's a ticklish thing to crawl over the stern of a canoe in the spatter of slugs, with the roar of muzzle-loaders above. It's shakin' to the nerves, but the maid never flinched, not even when a bullet split the gunnel. She ripped a piece of her dress and plugged a hole under the water line while I paddled out of range.

"The next winter at Holy Cross she ran to me shaking one day.

"'He is here! He is here! Oh, Big man, I am afraid!'

"'Who's here?' says I.

"'He is here - Father Orloff,' and her eyes was round and scared so that I took her up and kissed her while she clung to me - she was such a little girl.

"'He spoke to me at the water-hole, "I have come for you." I ran very fast, but he came behind. "Where is George?"' he said.

"I went out of the cabin down to the Mission, and into the house of Father Barnum. He was there.

"'Orloff! What do ye want?' I says.

"Father Barnum speaks up - 'he's known for a good man the length of the river. George,' says he, 'Father Orloff tells me you stole the girl Metla from her tribe. 'Tis a shameful thing for a white to take a red girl for his wife, but it's a crime to live as you do.'

"'What?' says I.

"'We can't sell you provisions nor allow you to stay in the village.'

"Orloff grins. 'You must go on,' he says, 'or give her up.'

"'No! I'll do neither.' And I shows the paper from the missionary at Nulato statin' that we were married. 'She's my wife,' says I, 'and too good for me. She's left her people and her gods, and I'll care for her.' I saw how it hurt Orloff, and I laid my hand on his shoulder close to the neck. 'I distrust ye, and sure as Fate ye'll die the shocking death if ever harm comes to the little one.'

"That was the winter of the famine, though every winter was the same then, and I went to Anvik for grub - took all the strong men and dogs in the village. I was afraid when I left, too, for 'twas the time I should have been with her, but there was no one else to go.

"'When you come back,' she said, 'there will be another - a little boy - and he will grow mighty and strong, like his father.' She hung her arms around me, Cap, and I left with her kisses warm on my lips.

"It was a terrible trip, the river wet with overflows and the cut-offs drifted deep, so I drove back into Holy Cross a week late with bleedin' dogs and frozen Indians strainin' at the sled ropes.

"I heard the wail of the old women before. I come to

the cabin, and when Metla had sobbed the story out in her weakness, I went back into the dark and down to the Mission. I remember how the Northern Lights flared over the hills above, and the little spruces on the summit looked to me like headstones, black against the moon - and I laughed when I saw the snow red in the night glare, for it meant blood and death.

"It was as lusty a babe as ever crowed, but Orloff had come to the sick bed and sent her squaws away. Baptism and such things he said he'd do. The little fellow died that night.

"They say the Mission door was locked and barred, but I pushed through it like paper and came into Father Barnum's house, where they sat. Fifty below is bad for the naked flesh. I broke in, bare-headed, mittenless, and I'd froze some on the way down. He saw murder in my eyes and tried to run, but I got him as he went out of the room. He tore his throat loose from my stiffened fingers and went into the church, but I beat down the door with my naked fists, mocking at his prayers inside, and may I never be closer to death than Orloff was that night.

"Then a squaw tugged at my parka.

"'She is dying, Anguk,' she said, and I ran back up the hill with the cold bitin' at my heart.

"There was no death that night in Holy Cross, though God knows one naked soul was due to walk out onto the snow. At daylight, when I came back for him, he had fled down the river with the fastest dogs, and to this day I've never seen his face, though 'tis often I've felt his hate.

"He's grown into the strongest missionary on the coast, and he never lets a chance go by to harry me or the girl.

"D'ye mind the time 'Skagway' Bennet died? We was pardners up Norton Sound way when he was killed. They thought he suicided, but I know. I found a cariboo belt in the brush near camp - the kind they make on the Kuskokwim, Father Orion's country. His men took the wrong one, that's all.

"I'm sorry I didn't tell ye this, Cap, before we started, for now we're into the South Country, where he owns the natives. He knows we've come, as the blood-token of the guide showed. He wants my life, and there's great trouble comin' up. I'm hopin' ye'll soon get your sight, for by now there's a runner twenty miles into the hills with news that we're blind in the church at Togiak. Three days he'll be goin', and on the fifth ye'll hear the jangle of Russian dog-bells. He'll kill the fastest team in Nushagak in the comin', and God help us if we're here."

George scraped a bit of frost-lace from the lone window pane. Dark figures moved over the snow, circling the chapel, and he knew that each was armed. Only their reverence for the church held them from doing the task set by Orloff, and he sighed as he changed the bandages on his suffering mate.

They awoke the next morning to the moan of wind and the sift of snow clouds past their walls. Staring through his peep-hole, George distinguished only a seethe of whirling flakes that greyed the view, blotting even the neighbouring huts, and when the early evening brought a rising note in the storm the trouble lifted from his face.

"A three-day blizzard," he rejoiced, "and the strongest team on the coast can't wallow through it under a week. These on-shore gales is beauts."

For three days the wind tore from off the sea into the open bight at whose head lay Togiak, and its violence wrecked the armour of shore ice in the bay till it beat and roared against the spit, a threshing maelstrom of shattered bergs. The waters piled into the inlet driven by the lash of the storm till they overflowed the river ice behind the village, submerging and breaking it into ragged, dangerous confusion.

On the third day, with Arctic vagary, the wind gasped reluctantly and scurried over the range. In its wake the surging ocean churned loudly and the back-water behind the town, held by the dam of freezing slush-ice at the river mouth, was skimmed by a thin ice-paper, pierced here and there by the up-ended piles from beneath. This held the night's snow, so that morning showed the village girt on three sides by a stream soft-carpeted and safe to the eye, but failing beneath the feet of a child.

"You're eyes are comin' along mighty slow," worried George. "I'm hopin' his reverence is up to his gills in drifts back yonder. "We must leave him a sled trail for a souvenir."

"How can we, with the place guarded?"

"Hitch the dogs and run for it by night, He'll burn us out when he comes. Fine targets we'd make on the snow by the light of a burning shack. If ye can see to shoot we'll go tonight. Hello! What's that?"

Outside came the howl of malamoots and the cry of men. Leaping to the window, George rubbed it free and stared into the sunshine.

"Too late! Too late!" he said. "Here he comes! It's time I killed him." He spoke gratingly, with the dull anger of years.

On the bright surface of the opposite hillside a sled bearing a muffled figure appeared silhouetted against the glisten of the crust. Its team, maddened by the village scent, poured down the incline toward the river bank and the guide swung onto the runners behind, while the voice of the people rose to their priest. In a whirl of soft snow they drove down onto the treachery of the ice. The screams of the natives frenzied the pack and they rioted out onto the bending sheet, while the long sledge, borne by its momentum, shot forward till the splitting cry of the ice sounded over the lamentations. It slackened, sagged and disappeared in a surge of congealing waters. The wheel dogs were dragged into the opening and their mates ahead jerked backward onto them. In a fighting tangle, all settled into the swirl.

Orloff leaped from the sinking sled, but hindered by his fur swaddling, crashed through and lunged heavily in his struggles to mount the edge of the film. As he floundered onto the caving surface it let him back and the waters covered him time and again. He pitched oddly about, and for the first time they saw his eyes were bound tightly with bandages, which he strove to loosen.

"My God! He's snow-blind!" cried George, and in a moment he appeared among the frantic mob fringing the shore.

The guide broke his way toward a hummock of old ice forming an islet near by, and the priest half swam, half scrambled behind, till they crawled out upon this solid footing. Here the wintry wind searched them and their dripping clothes stiffened quickly. Orloff dragged the strips from his face, and as the sun glitter pierced his eyes he writhed as though seared by the naked touch of hot steel.

He shouted affrightedly in his blindness, but the mocking voice of Big George answered him and he cowered at the malevolence in the words.

"Here I am, Orloff. It's help ye want, is it? I'll shoot the man that tries to reach ye. Ha, ha! You're freezin' eh? Georgie will talk to keep ye awake. A dirty trick of the river to cheat me so. I've fattened for years on the hope of stampin' your life out and now it's robbed me. But I'll stick till ye're safe in Hell."

The man cried piteously, turning his bleared eyes toward the sound.

"Shoot, why don't you, and end it? Can't you see we're freezing?" He stood up in his carapace of stiffened clothes, shivering palsiedly.

"The truest thing ye ever said," cried George, and he swung his colts into view. "It'll favour you and I'll keep my vow." He raised the gun. The splashing of the distant dogs broke the silence. A native knelt stiffly.

"George! George!" Captain had stumbled down among them and plucked at his arm, peering dimly into his distorted face. "Great God, are you a murderer? They'll be dead before we can save them."

"Save 'em ?" said George, while reason fought with his mania. "Whose goin' to save 'em? He needs killin'. I'm hungry for his life."

"He's a man, George. They're both human, and they're dying in sight of us. Give him a chance. Fight like a man."

As he spoke the fury fell away from the whaler and he became the alert, strong man of the frontier, knowing the quick danger and meeting it.

He bellowed at the natives and they fled backward before his voice, storming the cache where lay the big skin canoes. They slid one down and seizing paddles crushed the ice around it till it floated, then supported by the prow, George stamped the ice into fragments ahead, and they forced their way slowly along the channel he made. Soaked to the armpits he smashed a trail through which they reached the hummock where the others lay, too listless for action.

At the shore they bore the priest to their shelter while the guide was snatched into a near-by hut. They hacked off his brittle clothes and supported him to the bed. As he walked his feet clattered on the board floor like the sound of wooden shoes. They were white and solid, as were his hands.

"He's badly frozen," whispered Captain, "can we save him?" They rubbed and thawed for hours, but the sluggish blood refused to flow into the extremities and Captain felt that this man would die for lack of amputation.

Through all the Russian was silent, gazing strangely at George.

"'Tis no use," finally said the big man, despairingly, "I've seen too many of 'em; we've done our best."

He disappeared, and there sounded the jingle of harness as the dogs were hitched. As he entered for the camp outfit Orloff spoke:

"George Brace, I've harmed you bitterly these many years, and you're a good man to help me so. It's no use. We have both fought the Cold Death, and know when to quit. I came here to kill you, but you will go out across the mountains free, while I rave in madness and the medicine men make charms over me. When you come into Bethel Mission I'll be dead. Good-bye."

"Good Hell! We're takin' ye to Bethel and a doctor in ten minutes. A week's travel as the trail goes, but we'll save a chunk of ye yet, old man."

Five days later a broken team crawled over the snow to the Moravian Mission, urged by two men gaunt from the trail, and blistered by the cold. From the sledge came shrieks and throaty mutterings, horrid gabblings of post-freezing madness and Dr. Forrest, lifting back the robe, found Orloff lashed into his couch.

"Five days from Togiak. Two hundred miles in heavy trails," explained George wearily, as the cries of the maniac dimmed behind the log walls.

Two hours later Forrest spoke gravely as they nursed their frost bites in his room.

"We have operated. He will recover."

"It's a sad, sad day,'" mourned George. "It just takes the taste out of everything for me. He's a cripple now, eh ?"

"Yes! Helpless! I did not know Father Orloff had many - er - friends hereabout," continued the doctor. "He was thought to be hated by the whites. I'm glad the report was wrong."

"Friends be damned," said the other strongly. "What's a friend? Ye can get them any place, but where can ye find another enemy like that man?"

THE SCOURGE

Coming down coast from the Kotzebue country they stumbled onto the little camp in the early winter, and as there was food a plenty, of its kind, whereas they had subsisted for some days on puree of seal oil and short ribs of dog, Captain and Big George decided to winter. A maxim of the north teaches to cabin by a grub-pile.

It was an odd village they beheld that first day. Instead of the clean moss-chinked log shelters men were wont to build in this land, they found the community housed like marmots in holes and burrows.

It seemed that the troop had landed, fresh from the States, a hundred and a quarter strong, hot with the lust for gold, yet shaken by the newspaper horrors of Alaska's rigorous hardships and forbidding climate.

Debouching in the early fall, they had hastily prepared for an Associated Press-painted Arctic winter.

Had they been forced to winter in the mountains of Idaho, or among Montana's passes, they would have prepared simply and effectively. Here, however, in a mystic land, surrounded by the unknown, they grew panic stricken and lost their wits.

Thus, when the two "old timers" came upon them in the early winter they found them in bomb-proof hovels, sunk into the muck, banked with log walls, and thatched over with dirt and sod.

"Where are your windows and ventilators?" they were asked, and collectively the camp laughed at the question. *They* knew how to keep snug and warm even if half-witted "sourdoughs" didn't. *They* weren't taking any chances on freezing, not on your tin-type, no outdoor work and exposure for them!

As the winter settled, they snuggled back, ate three meals and more daily of bacon, beans, and baking-powder bread; playing cribbage for an appetite. They undertook no exercise more violent than seven-up, while the wood-cutting fell as a curse upon those unfortunates who lost at the game. They giggled at Captain and the big whaler who daily, snow or blow, hit the trail or wielded pick and shovel.

However, as the two maintained their practice, the camp grew to resent their industry, and, as is possible only in utterly idle communities, there sprung up a virulence totally out of proportion, and, founded without reason, most difficult to dispel. Before they knew it, the two were disliked and distrusted; their presence ignored; their society shunned.

Captain had talked to many in the camp. "You'll get scurvy, sure, living in these dark houses. They're damp and dirty, and you don't exercise. Besides, there isn't a pound of fresh grub in camp."

Figuratively, the camp's nose had tilted at this, and it stated pompously that it were better to preserve its classic purity of features and pro rata of toes, than to jeopardize these adjuncts through fear of a possible blood disease.

"Blood disease, eh?" George snorted like a sea-lion. "Wait till your legs get black and you spit your teeth out like plum-pits - mebbe you'll listen then. It'll come, see if it don't."

He was right. Yet when the plague did grip the camp and men died, one in five, they failed to rise to it. Instead of fighting manfully they lapsed into a frightened, stubborn coma.

There was one, and only one, who did not. Klusky the Jew; Klusky the pariah. They said he worked just to be ornery and different from the rest, he hated them so. They enjoyed baiting him to witness his fury. It sated that taint of Roman cruelty inherent in the man of ignorance. He was all the amusement they had, for it wasn't policy to stir up the two others - they might slop over and clean up the village. So they continued to goad him as they had done since leaving 'Frisco. They gibed and jeered till he shunned them, living alone in the fringe of the pines, bitter and vicious, as an outcast from the pack will grow, whether human or lupine. He frequented only the house of Captain and George, because they were exiles like himself.

The partners did not relish this overmuch, for he was an odious being, avaricious, carping, and dirty.

"His face reminds me of a tool," said George, once, "nose an' chin shuts up like calipers. He's got the forehead of a salmon trout, an' his chin don't retreat, it stampedes, plumb down ag'in his apple. Look out for that droop of the mouth. I've seen it before, an' his eyes is bad, too. They've stirred him up an' pickled all the good he ever had. Some day he'll do a murder."

"I wonder what he means by always saying he'll have revenge before spring. It makes me creep to hear him cackle and gloat. I think he's going crazy."

"Can't tell. This bunch would bust anybody's mental tugs, an' they make a mistake drivin' him so. Say! How's my gums look tonight?" George stretched his lips back, showing his teeth, while Captain made careful examination.

"All right. How are mine?"

"Red as a berry."

Every day they searched thus for the symptoms, looking for discolouration, and anxiously watching bruises on limb or body. Men live in fear when their comrades vanish silently from their midst. Each night upon retiring they felt legs nervously, punching here and there to see that the flesh retained its resiliency.

So insidious is the malady's approach that it may be detected only thus. A lassitude perhaps, a rheumatic laziness, or pains and swelling at the joints. Mayhap one notes a putty-like softness of the lower limbs. Where he presses, the finger mark remains, filling up sluggishly. No mental depression at first, nor fever, only a drooping ambition, fatigue, enlarging parts, now gradual, now sudden.

The grim humour of seeing grown men gravely poking their legs with rigid digits, or grinning anxiously into hand-mirrors had struck some of the tenderfeet at first, but the implacable progress of the disease; its black, merciless presence, pausing destructively here and there, had terrorized them into a hopeless fatalism till they cowered helplessly, awaiting its touch.

One night Captain announced to his partner. "I'm going over to the Frenchmen's, I hear Menard is down."

"What's the use of buttin' in where ye ain't wanted? As fer me, them frogeaters can all die like salmon; I won't go nigh 'em an' I've told 'em so. I give 'em good advice, an' what'd I get? What'd that daffy doctor do? Pooh-poohed at me an' physiced them. Lord! Physic a man with scurvy - might as well bleed a patient fer amputation." George spoke with considerable heat.

Captain pulled his parka hood well down so that the fox-tails around the edge protected his features, and stepped out into the evening. He had made several such trips in the past few months to call on men smitten with the sickness, but all to no effect. Being "chechakos" they were supreme in their conceit, and refused to heed his advice.

Returning at bed time he found his partner webbing a pair of snow-shoes by the light of a stinking "go-devil," consisting of a string suspended in a can of molten grease. The camp had sold them grub, but refused the luxury of candles. Noting his gravity, George questioned:

"Well, how's Menard?"

"Dead!" Captain shook himself as though at the memory. "It was awful. He died while I was talking

Rex E. Beach

to him."

"Don't say! How's that?"

"I found him propped up in a chair. He looked bad, but said he was feeling fine -"

"That's the way they go. I've seen it many a time - feelin' fine plumb to the last."

"He'd been telling me about a bet he had with Promont. Promont was taken last week, too, you know, same time. Menard bet him twenty dollars that he'd outlast him."

"'I'm getting all right,' says he, 'but poor Promont's going to die. I'll get his twenty, sure!' I turned to josh with the boy a bit, an' when I spoke to Menard he didn't answer. His jaw had sagged and he'd settled in his chair. Promont saw it, too, and cackled. 'H'I 'ave win de bet! H'I 'ave win de bet!' That's all. He just slid off. Gee! It was horrible."

George put by his work and swore, pacing the rough pole floor.

"Oh, the cussed fools! That makes six dead from the one cabin - six from eighteen, an' Promont'll make seven to-morrow. Do ye mind how we begged 'em to quit that dug-out an' build a white man's house, an' drink spruce tea, an' _work_! They're too - lazy. They lie around in that hole, breath bad air, an' rot."

"And just to think, if we only had a crate of potatoes in camp we could save every man jack of 'em. Lord! They never even brought no citric acid nor lime juice -

nothin'! If we hadn't lost our grub when the whale-boat upset, eh? That ten-gallon keg of booze would help some. Say! I got such a thirst I don't never expect to squench it proper;" he spoke plaintively.

"Klusky was here again while you was gone, too. I itch to choke that Jew whenever he gets to ravin' over these people. He's sure losin' his paystreak. He gritted his teeth an' foamed like a mad malamoot, I never see a low-downer lookin' aspect than him when he gets mad."

"'I'll make 'em come to me,' says he, 'on their bellies beggin'. It ain't time yet. Oh, no! Wait 'till half of 'em is dead, an' the rest is rotten with scurvy. Then they'll crawl to me with their gums thick and black, an' their flesh like dough; they'll kiss my feet an' cry, an' I'll stamp 'em into the snow!' You'd ought a heard him laugh. Some day I'm goin' to lay a hand on that man, right in my own house."

As they prepared for bed. Captain remarked:

"By the way, speaking of potatoes, I heard to-night that there was a crate in the Frenchmen's outfit somewhere, put in by mistake. perhaps, but when they boated their stuff up river last fall it couldn't be found - must have been lost."

It was some days later that, returning from a gameless hunt, Captain staggered into camp, weary from the drag of his snow-shoes.

Throwing himself into his bunk he rested while George prepared the meagre meal of brown beans, fried salt pork, and sour-dough bread. The excellence of this last, due to the whaler's years of practice, did much to mitigate the unpleasantness of the milkless, butterless, sugarless menu.

Captain's fatigue prevented notice of the other's bearing. However, when he had supped and the dishes were done George spoke, quietly and without emotion.

"Well, boy, the big thing has come off."

"What do you mean?"

For reply he took the grease dip and, holding it close, bared his teeth.

With a cry Captain leaped from his bunk, and took his face between his hands.

"Great God! George!"

He pushed back the lips. Livid blotches met his gaze - the gums swollen and discoloured. He dropped back sick and pale, staring at his bulky comrade, dazed and uncomprehending.

Carefully replacing the lamp, George continued:

"I felt it comin' quite a while back, pains in my knees an' all that - thought mebbe you'd notice me hobblin' about. I can't git around good - feel sort of stove up an' spavined on my feet."

"Yes, yes, but we've lived clean, and exercised, and drank spruce tea, and - everything," cried the other.

"I know, but I've had a touch before; it's in my blood I

reckon. Too much salt grub; too many winters on the coast. She never took me so sudden an' vicious though. Guess the stuff's off."

"Don't talk that way," said Captain, sharply. "You're not going to die - I won't let you."

"Vat's the mattaire?" came a leering voice and, turning they beheld Klusky, the renegade. He had entered silently, as usual, and now darted shrewd inquiring glances at them.

"George has the scurvy."

"Oi! Oi! Oi! Vat a peety." He seemed about to say more but refrained, coming forward rubbing his hands nervously.

"It ain't possible that a 'sour dough' shall have the scoivy."

"Well, he has it - has it bad but I'll cure him. Yes, and I'll save this whole - camp, whether they want it or not." Captain spoke strongly, his jaws set with determination. Klusky regarded him narrowly through close shrunk eyes, while speculation wrinkled his low forehead.

"Of course! Yes! But how shall it be, eh? Tell me that." His eagerness was pronounced.

"I'll go to St. Michaels and bring back fresh grub."

"You can't do it, boy," said George. "It's too far an' there ain't a dog in camp. You couldn't haul your outfit alone, an' long before you'd sledded grub back I'd be wearin' one of them gleamin' orioles, I believe that's what they call it, on my head, like the pictures of them little fat angelettes. I ain't got no ear for music, so I'll have to cut out the harp solos."

"Quit that talk, will you?" said Captain irritably. "Of course, one man can't haul an outfit that far, but two can, so I'm going to take Klusky with me." He spoke with finality, and the Jew started, gazing queerly. "We'll go light, and drive back a herd of reindeer."

"By thunder! I'd clean forgot the reindeer. The government was aimin' to start a post there last fall, wasn't it? Say! Mebbe you can make it after all, Kid." His features brightened hopefully. "What d' ye say, Klusky?"

The one addressed answered nervously, almost with excitement.

"It can't be done! It ain't possible, and I ain't strong enough to pull the sled. V'y don't you and George go together. I'll stay -"

Captain laid a heavy hand on his shoulder.

"That'll do. What are you talking about? George wouldn't last two days, and you know it. Now listen. You don't have to go, you infernal greasy dog, there are others in camp, and one of them will go if I walk him at the muzzle of a gun. I gave you first chance, because we've been good to you. Now get out."

He snatched him from his seat and hurled him at the door, where he fell in a heap.

Klusky arose, and, although his eyes snapped wildly and he trembled, he spoke insidiously, with oily modulation.

"Vait a meenute, Meestaire Captain, vait a meenute. I didn't say I vouldn't go. Oi! Oi! Vat a man! Shoor I'll go. Coitenly! You have been good to me and they have been devils. I hope they die." He shook a bony fist in the direction of the camp, while his voice took on its fanatical shrillness. "They shall be in h - before I help them, the pigs, but you - ah, you have been my friends, yes ?"

"All right; be here at daylight," said Captain gruffly. Anger came slowly to him, and its trace was even slower in its leaving.

"I don't like him," said George, when he had slunk out. "He ain't on the level. Watch him close, boy, he's up to some devilment."

"Keep up your courage, old man. I'll be back in twelve days." Captain said it with decision, though his heart sank as he felt the uncertainties before him.

George looked squarely into his eyes.

"God bless ye, boy," he said. "I've cabined with many a man, but never one like you. I'm a hard old nut, an' I ain't worth what you're goin' to suffer, but mebbe you can save these other idiots. That's what we're put here for, to help them as is too ornery to help theirselves." He smiled at Captain, and the young man left him blindly. He seldom smiled, and to see it now made his partner's breast heave achingly.

"Good old George!" he murmured as they pulled out upon the river. "Good old George!" As they passed from the settlement an Indian came to the door of the last hovel.

"Hello. There's a Siwash in your cabin," said Captain. "What is he doing there ?"

"That's all right," rejoined Klusky. "I told him to stay and vatch t'ings."

"Rather strange," thought the other. "I wonder what there is to watch. There's never been any stealing around here."

To the unversed, a march by sled would seem simplicity. In reality there is no more discouraging test than to hit the trail, dogless and by strength of back. The human biped cannot drag across the snow for any distance more than its own weight; hence equipment is of the simplest. At that, the sledge rope galls one's neck with a continual, endless, yielding drag, resulting in back pains peculiar to itself. It is this eternal maddening pull, with the pitiful crawling gait that tells; horse's labour and a snail's pace. The toil begets a perspiration which the cold solidifies midway through the garments. At every pause the clammy clothes grow chill, forcing one forward, onward, with sweating body and freezing face. In extreme cold, snow pulverizes dryly till steel runners drag as though slid through sand. Occasional overflows bar the stream from bank to bank, resulting in wet feet and quick changes by hasty fires to save numb toes. Now the air is dead under a smother of falling flakes that fluff up ankle deep, knee deep, till the sled plunges along behind, half buried, while the men wallow and invent ingenious oaths. Again the wind whirls it by in grotesque goblin shapes; wonderful storm beings, writhing, whipping, biting as they pass; erasing bank and mountain. Yet always there is that aching, steady tug of the shoulder-rope, stopping circulation till the arms depend numbly; and always the weary effort of trail breaking.

Captain felt that he had never worked with a more unsatisfying team mate. Not that Klusky did not pull, he evidently did his best, but he never spoke, while the other grew ever conscious of the beady, glittering eyes boring into his back. At camp, the Jew watched him furtively, sullenly, till he grew to feel oppressed, as with a sense of treachery, or some fell design hidden far back. Every morning he secured the ropes next the sled, thus forcing Captain to walk ahead. He did not object to the added task of breaking trail, for he had expected the brunt of the work, but the feeling of suspicion increased till it was only by conscious effort that he drove himself to turn his back upon the other and take up the journey.

It was this oppression that warned him on the third day. Leaning as he did against the sled ropes he became aware of an added burden, as though the man behind had eased to shift his harness. When it did not cease he glanced over his shoulder. Keyed up as he was this nervous agility saved him.

Klusky held a revolver close up to his back, and, though he had unconsciously failed to pull, he mechanically stepped in the other's tracks. The courage to shoot had failed him momentarily, but as Captain turned, it came, and he pulled the trigger.

Frozen gun oil has caused grave errors in calculation. The hammer curled back wickedly and stuck. Waiting his chance he had carried the weapon in an outer pocket where the frost had stiffened the grease. Had it been warmed next his body, the fatal check would not have occurred. Even so, he pulled again and it exploded sharp and deafening in the rarefied morning air. In that instant's pause, however, Captain had whirled so that the bullet tore through the loose fur beneath his arm. He struck, simultaneously with the report, and the gun flew outward, disappearing in the snow.

They grappled and fell, rolling in a tangle of rope, Klusky fighting with rat-like fury, whining odd, broken curses. The larger man crushed him in silence, beating him into the snow, bent on killing him with his hands.

As the other's struggles diminished, he came to himself, however, and desisted.

"I can't kill him," he thought in panic. "I can't go on alone."

"Get up!" He kicked the bleeding figure till it arose lamely. "Why did you do that?" His desire to strangle the life from him was over-powering.

The man gave no answer, muttering only unintelligible jargon, his eyes ablaze with hatred.

"Tell me." He shook him by the throat but received no reply. Nor could he, try as he pleased; only a stubborn silence. At last, disgusted and baffled, he bade him resume the rope. It was necessary to use force for this, but eventually they took up the journey, differing now only in their order of precedence.

"If you make a move I'll knife you," he cautioned grimly. "That goes for the whole trip, too."

At evening he searched the grub kit, breaking knives and forks, and those articles which might be used as means of offence, throwing the pieces into the snow.

"Don't stir during the night, or I might kill you. I wake easy, and hereafter we'll sleep together." Placing the weapons within his shirt, he bound the other's wrists and rolled up beside him.

Along the coast, their going became difficult from the rough ice and soft snow, and with despair Captain felt the days going by. Klusky maintained his muteness and, moreover, to the anger of his captor, began to shirk. It became necessary to beat him. This Captain did relentlessly, deriving a certain satisfaction from it, yet marvelling the while at his own cruelty. The Jew feigned weariness, and began to limp as though footsore.

Captain halted him at last.

"Don't try that game," he said. "It don't go. I spared your life for a purpose. The minute you stop pulling, that minute I'll sink this into your ribs." He prodded him with his sheath knife. "Get along now, or I'll make you haul it alone." He kicked him into resentful motion again, for he had come to look upon him as an animal, and was heedless of his signs of torture - so thus they marched; master and slave. "He's putting it on," he thought, but abuse as he might, the other's efforts became weaker, and his agony more marked as the days passed.

The morning came when he refused to arise.

"Get up!"

Klusky shook his head.

"Get up, I say!" Captain spoke fiercely, and snatched him to foot, but with a groan the man sank back. Then, at last, he talked.

"I can't do it. I can't do it. My legs make like they von't vork. You can kill me, but I can't valk."

As he ceased, Captain leaned down and pushed back his lips. The teeth were loose and the gums livid.

"Great Heavens, what have I done! *What have I done*!" he muttered.

Klusky had watched his face closely.

"Vat's the mattaire? Vy do you make like that, eh? Tell me." His voice was sharp.

"You've got it."

"I've got it? Oi! Oi! I've got it! Vat have I got?" He knew before the answer came, but raved and cursed in frenzied denial. His tongue started, language flowed from him freely.

"It ain't that. No! No! It is the rheumatissen. Yes, it shall be so. It makes like that from the hard vork always. It is the cold - the cold makes it like."

With despair Captain realized that he could neither go on, dragging the sick man and outfit, nor could he stay here in idleness to sacrifice the precious days that remained to his partner. Each one he lost might mean life or death.

Klusky broke in upon him.

"You von't leave me, Mistaire Captain? Please you von't go avay?"

Such frightened entreaty lay in his request that before thinking the other replied.

"No, I won't. I made you come and I'll do all I can for you. Maybe somebody will pass." He said it only to cheer, for no one travelled this miserable stretch save scattering, half-starved Indians, but the patient caught at it eagerly, hugging the hope to his breast during the ensuing days.

That vigil beside the dying creature lived long in Captain's memory. The bleak, timberless shores of the bay; their tiny tent, crouched fearfully among the willow tops; the silent nights, when in the clear, cold air the stars stared at him close and big, like eyes of wolves beyond a camp fire; the days of endless gabblings from the sinking man, and the all pervading cold.

At last, knowledge dawned upon the invalid, and he called his companion to his side. Shivering there beneath the thin tent, Captain heard a story, rambling at first, filled with hatred and bitterness toward the men who had scoffed at him, yet at the last he listened eagerly, amazedly, and upon its conclusion rose suddenly, gazing at the dying man in horror.

"My God, Klusky! Hell isn't black enough for you. It can't be true, it can't be. You're raving! Do you mean to say that you let those poor devils die like rats while you had potatoes in your cabin, fresh ones? Man! Man! The juice of every potato was worth a life. You're lying, Klusky."

"I ain't. No, I ain't. I hate them! I said they should crawl on their bellies to me. Yes, and I should wring the money out. A hundred dollars for von potato. I stole them all. Ha! ha! and I kept them varm. Oh, yes! Alvays varm by the fire, so they shall be good and fine for the day."

"That's why you left the Indian there when we came away, eh? To keep a fire."

"Shoor! and I thought I shall kill you and go back alone so nobody shall make for the rescue. Then I should have the great laugh."

Captain bared his head to the cold outside the tent. He was dazed by the thought of it. The man was crazed by abuse. The camp had paid for its folly!

Then a hope sprang up in him. It was too late to go on and return with the deer; that is, too late for George, and he thought only of him; of the big, brave man sitting alone in the cabin, shunned by the others, waiting quietly for his coming, tracing the relentless daily march of the disease. Why didn't the Jew die so he could flee back? He had promised not to desert him, and he could not break his word to a dying man, even though the wretch deserved damnation. But why couldn't he die? What made him hang on so? In his idle hours he arranged a pack for the start, assembling his rations. He could not be hampered by the sled. This was to be a race - he must travel long and fast. The sick man saw the preparations, and cried weakly, the tears freezing on his cheeks, and still he lingered, lingered maddeningly, till at last, when Captain had lost count of the days, he passed without a twitch and, before the body had cooled, the northward bluffs hid the plodding, snow-shoed figure hurrying along the back trail.

He scarcely stopped for sleep or food, but gnawed raw bacon and frozen bread, swinging from shoe to shoe, devouring distance with the steady, rhythmic pace of a machine. He made no fires. As darkness settled, rendering progress a peril, he unrolled his robe, and burrowed into some overhanging drift, and the earliest hint of dawn found him miles onward.

Though the weather was clear, he grew numbed and careless under the strain of his fatigue, so that the frost bit hungrily at his features. He grew gaunt, and his feet swelled from the snow-shoe thongs till they puffed out his loose, sealskin boots, and every step in the morning hours brought forth a groan.

He was tortured by the thought that perhaps the Indian had carelessly let go the fire in Klusky's cabin. If so, the precious potatoes would freeze in a night. Then, if the native rebuilt it, he would arrive only to find a mushy, putrifying mass, worse than useless. The uncertainty sickened him, and at last, as he sighted the little hamlet, he paused, bracing his legs apart weakly.

He searched fearfully for traces of smoke above

Klusky's cabin. There were none. Somehow the lone shack seemed to stare malignantly at him, as he staggered up the trail, and he heard himself muttering. There were no locks in this land, so he entered unbidden. The place was empty, though warm from recent habitation. With his remaining strength he scrambled up a rude ladder to the loft where he fumbled in the dark while his heart stopped. Then he cried hoarsely and, ripping open the box, stuffed them gloatingly into pockets and shirt front. He dropped from the platform and fled out through the open door, capless and mittenless; out and on toward the village.

His pace slackened suddenly, for he noted with a shock that, like Klusky's cabin, no smoke drifted over the house toward which he ran, and, drawing near, he saw that snow lay before the door; clean, white, and untrodden. He was too dazed to recall the light fall of the night previous, but glared blankly at the idle pipe; at the cold and desolate front.

"Too late!" he murmured brokenly. "Too late!" and stumbled to the snow-cushioned chopping block.

He dared not go in. Evidently the camp had let George die; had never come near to lift a hand. He was afraid of what lay within, afraid to face it alone. Yet a dreadful need to know pulled him forward. Three times he approached the door, retreating each time in panic. At last he laid soft hands upon the latch and entered, averting his eyes. Even so, and despite the darkness inside, he was conscious of it; saw from his eye corners the big, still bulk that sat wrapped and propped in the chair by the table. He sensed it dazedly, inductively, and turned to flee, then paused.

"Ye made it, boy! It's the twelfth to-day." George's voice came weakly, and with a great cry Captain sprang to him.

"Bout all in," the other continued. "Ain't been on my feet for two days. I knowed you'd come to-day, though; it's the twelfth."

Captain made no reply, for he had knelt, his face buried in the big man's lap, his shoulders heaving, while he cried like a little boy.

Choose from Thousands of 1stWorldLibrary Classics By

Adolphus WilliamWard
Aesop
Agatha Christie
Alexander Aaronsohn
Alexander Kielland
Alexandre Dumas
Alfred Gatty
Alfred Ollivant
Alice Duer Miller
Alice Turner Curtis
Alice Dunbar
Ambrose Bierce
Amelia E. Barr
Andrew Lang
Andrew McFarland Davis
Anna Sewell
Annie Besant
Annie Hamilton Donnell
Annie Payson Call
Anton Chekhov
Arnold Bennett
Arthur Conan Doyle
Arthur Ransome
Atticus
B. M. Bower
Basil King
Bayard Taylor
Ben Macomber
Booth Tarkington
Bram Stoker
C. Collodi
C. E. Orr
C. M. Ingleby
Carolyn Wells
Catherine Parr Traill
Charles A. Eastman
Charles Dickens
Charles Dudley Warner
Charles Farrar Browne
Charles Ives
Charles Kingsley
Charles Lathrop Pack
Charles Whibley
Charles Willing Beale
Charlotte M. Braeme
Charlotte M.Yonge
Clair W. Hayes
Clarence Day Jr.
Clarence E. Mulford

Clemence Housman
Confucius
Cornelis DeWitt Wilcox
Cyril Burleigh
D. H. Lawrence
Daniel Defoe
David Garnett
Don Carlos Janes
Donald Keyhole
Dorothy Kilner
Dougan Clark
E. Nesbit
E.P.Roe
E. Phillips Oppenheim
Edgar Allan Poe
Edgar Rice Burroughs
Edith Wharton
Edward J. O'Biren
John Cournos
Edwin L. Arnold
Eleanor Atkins
Elizabeth Cleghorn
Gaskell
Elizabeth Von Arnim
Ellem Key
Emily Dickinson
Erasmus W. Jones
Ernie Howard Pie
Ethel Turner
Ethel Watts Mumford
Eugenie Foa
Eugene Wood
Evelyn Everett-Green
Everard Cotes
F. J. Cross
Federick Austin Ogg
Ferdinand Ossendowski
Francis Bacon
Francis Darwin
Frances Hodgson Burnett
Frank Gee Patchin
Frank Harris
Frank Jewett Mather
Frank L. Packard
Frederick Trevor Hill
Frederick Winslow Taylor
Friedrich Kerst
Friedrich Nietzsche
Fyodor Dostoyevsky

Gabrielle E. Jackson
Garrett P. Serviss
Gaston Leroux
George Ade
Geroge Bernard Shaw
George Ebers
George Eliot
George MacDonald
George Orwell
George Tucker
George W. Cable
George Wharton James
Gertrude Atherton
Grace E. King
Grant Allen
Guillermo A. Sherwell
Gulielma Zollinger
Gustav Flaubert
H. A. Cody
H. B. Irving
H. G. Wells
H. H. Munro
H. Irving Hancock
H. Rider Haggard
H. W. C. Davis
Hamilton Wright Mabie
Hans Christian Andersen
Harold Avery
Harold McGrath
Harriet Beecher Stowe
Harry Houidini
Helent Hunt Jackson
Helen Nicolay
Hendy David Thoreau
Henrik Ibsen
Henry Adams
Henry Ford
Henry Frost
Henry James
Henry Jones Ford
Henry Seton Merriman
Henry Wadsworth
Longfellow
Henry W Longfellow
Herbert A. Giles
Herbert N. Casson
Herman Hesse
Homer
Honore De Balzac

Horace Walpole
Horatio Alger, Jr.
Howard Pyle
Howard R. Garis
Hugh Lofting
Hugh Walpole
Humphry Ward
Ian Maclaren
Israel Abrahams
J.G.Austin
J. Henri Fabre
J. M. Barrie
J. Macdonald Oxley
J. S. Knowles
J. Storer Clouston
Jack London
Jacob Abbott
James Allen
James Lane Allen
James Andrews
James Baldwin
James DeMille
James Joyce
James Oliver Curwood
James Oppenheim
James Otis
Jane Austen
Jens Peter Jacobsen
Jerome K. Jerome
John Burroughs
John F. Kennedy
John Gay
John Glasworthy
John Habberton
John Joy Bell
John Milton
John Philip Sousa
Jonathan Swift
Joseph Carey
Joseph Conrad
Joseph Jacobs
Julian Hawthrone
Julies Vernes
Justin Huntly McCarthy
Kakuzo Okakura
Kenneth Grahame
Kate Langley Bosher
L. A. Abbot
L. T. Meade
L. Frank Baum
Laura Lee Hope

Laurence Housman
Leo Tolstoy
Leonid Andreyev
Lewis Carroll
Lilian Bell
Lloyd Osbourne
Louis Tracy
Louisa May Alcott
Lucy Fitch Perkins
Lucy Maud Montgomery
Lydia Miller Middleton
Lyndon Orr
M. H. Adams
Margaret E. Sangster
Margaret Vandercook
Maria Edgeworth
Maria Thompson Daviess
Mariano Azuela
Marion Polk Angellotti
Mark Overton
Mark Twain
Mary Austin
Mary Cole
Mary Rowlandson
Mary Wollstonecraft
Shelley
Max Beerbohm
Myra Kelly
Nathaniel Hawthrone
O. F. Walton
Oscar Wilde
Owen Johnson
P.G.Wodehouse
Paul and Mable Thorn
Paul G. Tomlinson
Paul Severing
Peter B. Kyne
Plato
R. Derby Holmes
R. L. Stevenson
Rabindranath Tagore
Rahul Alvares
Ralph Waldo Emmerson
Rene Descartes
Rex E. Beach
Richard Harding Davis
Richard Jefferies
Robert Barr
Robert Frost
Robert Gordon Anderson
Robert L. Drake

Robert Lansing
Robert Michael Ballantyne
Robert W. Chambers
Rosa Nouchette Carey
Ross Kay
Rudyard Kipling
Samuel B. Allison
Samuel Hopkins Adams
Sarah Bernhardt
Selma Lagerlof
Sherwood Anderson
Sigmund Freud
Standish O'Grady
Stanley Weyman
Stella Benson
Stephen Crane
Stewart Edward White
Stijn Streuvels
Swami Abhedananda
Swami Parmananda
T. S. Ackland
The Princess Der Ling
Thomas A. Janvier
Thomas A Kempis
Thomas Anderton
Thomas Bailey Aldrich
Thomas Bulfinch
Thomas De Quincey
Thomas H. Huxley
Thomas Hardy
Thomas More
Thornton W. Burgess
U. S. Grant
Valentine Williams
Victor Appleton
Virginia Woolf
Walter Scott
Washington Irving
Wilbur Lawton
Wilkie Collins
Willa Cather
Willard F. Baker
William Makepeace
Thackeray
William W. Walter
Winston Churchill
Yei Theodora Ozaki
Young E. Allison
Zane Grey